THE PRAIRIE CHICKEN KILL

Other Walker Mysteries by Bill Crider

The Truman Smith Series
Dead on the Island
Gator Kill
When Old Men Die

The Professor Carl Burns Series
A Dangerous Thing
One Dead Dean
Dying Voices

THE PRAIRIE CHICKEN KILL

A Truman Smith Mystery

Bill Crider

WALKER AND COMPANY
New York

First published in the United States of America in 1996 by Walker
Publishing Company, Inc.

Published simultaneously in Canada by Thomas Allen & Son Canada
Limited, Markham, Ontario

Library of Congress Cataloging-in-Publication Data
Crider, Bill, 1941–
The prairie chicken kill: a Truman Smith mystery/Bill Crider.
p. cm.
"A Walker mystery."
ISBN 0-8027-3282-8 (hardcover)
I. Title.
PS3553.R497P73

1996
813′.54—dc20   96-4009
CIP

Printed in the United States of America
2 4 6 8 10 9 7 5 3

To Charles and Marie Ferguson—
thanks for the trip to the Attwater
Prairie Chicken
National Wildlife Refuge

THE PRAIRIE CHICKEN KILL

1

I WAS SITTING on the frayed plastic webbing of my only aluminum lawn chair reading an old paperback copy of *Tobacco Road* when Dino drove up in a 1981 Pontiac Bonneville that was the color of the foam on top of a Gulf wave.

He stopped the car, got out, and crunched across the oystershell drive to where I was sitting in the shade of one of the dark green oleander bushes that surrounded my house. Dino's house really, but he was letting me live there.

Nameless, the big orange tomcat who shared the house with me, slipped out from under the bush where he'd been chasing a gecko and clawed at Dino's pants' leg.

"I think he's beginning to warm up to me," Dino said.

Nameless sat back and looked up at him, green-eyed and expectant. "Mowrr?" he said.

"He thinks you're here to feed him," I said, slipping the business card I used for a bookmark into *Tobacco Road* and closing the book. "Just about the only time you come by is when I'm not here and you're taking care of him."

Dino looked around uneasily. He didn't like being out of

his house, where he spent most of his time watching television. For a while he'd been hooked on the soaps and then on talk shows, but now that the local cable franchise had added a twenty-four-hour infomercial channel, he watched it almost constantly.

"Let's go inside," he said. "It's hot out here."

It was a typical Sunday afternoon in spring on the Texas coast, warm and only slightly muggy. There was a breeze from the Gulf stirring the oleander leaves and pushing along the puffy, flat-bottomed clouds overhead.

"It's not so bad," I said.

"Maybe not, but I need a place to sit down."

It wasn't that he needed a place to sit, any more than it was the heat. It was just that Dino was never comfortable unless he was inside, and he was only marginally comfortable inside unless he was in his own house.

I stuck the book under my arm and stood up.

"You read some funny stuff," Dino said.

"Some of it's pretty funny," I said, taking out the book and looking at the cover. "But not all of it."

"You know what I mean. I bet there's nobody else in the whole country reading that book right now."

He was probably right. Not too many people cared about Erskine Caldwell these days. Maybe that was why I was reading the book.

"It was considered pretty hot stuff at one time," I said.

"When was that?"

"A long time ago. Let's go in."

We went inside, and Nameless followed in the hope that someone might give him something to eat. It wouldn't have mattered if he'd eaten only ten minutes before; he was always ready to eat again if he got the chance.

"I'll feed you later," I told him, and he flopped down by my ratty sofa and started grooming himself, licking under his front paw and then dragging the paw across his face.

"You want a Big Red?" I asked Dino.

"Is that all you have? Jesus, Tru, don't you know that stuff'll kill you? I know this guy who works for the distributor, and he tells me that they never keep it around the warehouse for very long after it goes in the can. He said it eats right through the aluminum."

"If my stomach were lined with aluminum, I'd be worried. I've got ginger ale, though, if you want it."

"I guess that'll have to do."

The house was furnished in Early Thrift Shop. Dino sat in a recliner that wouldn't recline, and I went into the kitchen. Nameless got up, stretched, and followed me.

"How about turning on the air?" Dino yelled.

I didn't use the air-conditioning much. The house was made of stone and surrounded by oleander bushes, and there was always a breeze blowing in from the Gulf through the open windows. Dino would have felt better if the windows were closed.

"I couldn't afford to pay the electric bill if I ran the air," I said, laying my book on the counter and opening the refrigerator.

I had two liters of Big Red in a plastic bottle. As far as I could tell, it hadn't eaten its way through the plastic yet; there were no telltale red spots on the bottom of the refrigerator. Well, to tell the truth, there *were* a couple of red spots, but I figured them for rust.

The ginger ale was in green-and-white cans. They weren't leaking, either. I poured some Big Red in a glass and popped open one of the cans of ginger ale for Dino.

Nameless was watching me hopefully. He said, "Mowrr?"

"I told you I'd feed you later," I said.

He followed me back into the living room. I handed Dino his drink and sat on the sofa. A spring gave a muffled twang, but it didn't break through the cushion. Nameless sat by my foot and resumed his grooming, a process that could last for as little as ten seconds or as long as a quarter of an hour, depending on when he fell asleep.

"You didn't have a glass for me?" Dino asked.

"I washed off the top of the can," I lied. "It's clean."

He looked at the can suspiciously and took a sip of the ginger ale. Then he made a face and said, "I wish you had something a little stronger."

"I thought you liked to stay in shape."

"I do. I got me one of those Health Riders and an Ab-Flex. My gut's like iron. A little whiskey wouldn't hurt me."

He did look fit, his shoulders broad and his stomach flat. He was probably right about the whiskey not hurting him, but I didn't have any. Big Red was about as wild as I got.

"So why are you here?" I asked him. "Nameless doesn't need you to feed him, and you're not exactly in the habit of making social calls."

He set the ginger ale can on top of the low coffee table I'd bought at a garage sale. "Maybe I'm changing my habits. Maybe I just wanted to come by, see my old buddy Truman, see if he's doing all right. Maybe I wanted to see your stupid cat."

"I doubt it," I said without making any attempt to defend Nameless's intelligence. Nameless didn't care; he was already asleep, his head turned to one side, his paw thrown over his eye. "I hope it's not like the last time you came looking for me."

"When was that?"

He knew very well when that had been, but I said, "When Outside Harry disappeared."

"Oh. Yeah." He picked up the ginger ale can and took a swallow.

"Evelyn was with you that time. How's she doing?"

"She's doing great. We get together a couple of times a week now, go out and have some laughs."

I tried to imagine that. I couldn't.

"Where do you go?"

"Just around. We went to Moody Gardens and saw that 3-D IMAX movie, the one they filmed underwater. It was like the fish were swimming in my lap."

I couldn't picture Dino at Moody Gardens or anywhere else in Galveston, but maybe he was actually getting better about leaving his house.

"You didn't come here to tell me about the movie, though, did you?"

"Hey, you like to fish. You oughta go see it. That cat of yours would love it."

For just a second or two I had an image of Nameless sitting in my lap and wearing a specially-made little pair of wraparound polarized glasses. I smiled, and Dino said, "What's so funny?"

"Nothing." I swirled what was left of my Big Red around in the bottom of my glass. "Now why don't you tell me what you came out here for."

"Geez, Tru, can't we just have a little conversation, like old times?"

"Sure we can. Later, maybe. But right now you might as well get to the point."

He sighed and set the ginger ale can back on the coffee table. "All right. I got a call today from Lance Garrison. He wants to talk to you."

"Lance Garrison wants to talk to me?" That was about as likely as Nameless in 3-D glasses. Garrison and I hadn't seen each other or spoken in more than twenty years. "What about?"

"He didn't say. He just asked me if I'd bring you by his house this afternoon."

"I'm not going to find anybody for him if that's what he wants."

Finding people had been my job once, and sometimes

people still asked me to do it. I'd come back to Galveston a few years ago to find my sister, and it hadn't worked out. I didn't like to find people anymore.

"I don't know what he wants," Dino said. "I owe him a favor or two, so I said I'd ask you."

"I never liked him much."

"He knows that. That's why he called me instead of you. You gonna go with me or not?"

I thought about it for a second. "I went looking for Outside Harry because you asked me to. It didn't turn out so well."

"Hey, it turned out all right. Besides, Lance probably doesn't want you to find anybody. Maybe he just wants to talk over old times."

"Not with me, he doesn't."

Dino stood up. "OK. I asked, and you turned me down. I don't blame you. I never liked Lance much, myself."

"He made you some money, though, I hear."

"Who told you that?"

"It's just one of those things people talk about," I said. "Is it true?"

"Yeah, it's true. That's why I owe him a favor or two."

"All right," I said. "I'll talk to him."

"But you won't look for anybody, right?"

"Right."

"I don't blame you," Dino said.

2

LANCE GARRISON HAD done the one thing that no real Galvestonian could forgive him for: He'd been Born on the Island, but he'd moved to Houston and gotten rich.

That wasn't why I didn't like him, but there were plenty of others who held it against him. After all, the animosity between Galveston and Houston went back more than a hundred years. Galveston had been the jewel of the Gulf Coast in the nineteenth century, but after Houston dug a ship channel to the Gulf, Galveston went into a decline that in some ways continued even now.

That was just fine with me. There was a genteelly seedy charm to Galveston that Houston could never match; its traffic-choked freeways and its smoggy skies give it all the ambience of a backroom poker game at a life-insurance sales convention. You had to feel sorry for a place like that, not hate it. Other BOIs didn't see it that way, however. They hated Houston and always would.

When he got out of college, Lance Garrison found a job with a brokerage firm there and discovered that he had a real knack for picking stocks that were ready to explode. His clients started making money, real money, and they made it fast. Lance was investing right along with them, beginning with Wal-Mart before anyone else had heard of it, and a software company that now dominated the market.

He'd done so well that he'd owned a chunk of the Houston Astros at one time, then sold it for a large profit. But his smartest move recently had been to invest heavily in a Houston-based computer firm that had outdistanced IBM and nearly everyone else in the PC field.

How long a winning streak like Lance's could last was anyone's guess, but it had been going on for so many years now that no one really thought it would ever end. The rumor on the Island was that he'd made so much money that he wouldn't have time to spend it all even if he lived forever.

And as if that weren't bad enough, he'd done something even worse. He'd moved back to Galveston.

He hadn't moved back as a resident, though. That was the bad part. Instead, he'd built a weekend home in one of the upscale developments on the western end of the Island, where the streets had names like Jolly Roger Lane and Cross-bones Avenue. There wasn't a Tobacco Road anywhere in the bunch.

Sometimes the people who owned these homes jokingly called them "bait camps," as if they were places out of the Island's past, places that smelled of shrimp and mullet and squid, where the floors and cabinets were slippery with fish scales and blood, where there were no screens on the doors or windows to impede the breeze or the mosquitoes, and where you had to watch your step to avoid crunching the shells of the hermit crabs that scuttled across floors gritty with sand tracked in from the beach.

The houses weren't like that at all, of course. There were pseudo Victorian houses, pseudo Queen Anne houses, and houses that would look right at home on the shores of the Mediterranean; there were houses in a southwestern style straight from Santa Fe, and there were houses that looked as if they might have been flown in intact from French wine country. They were all built up on stilts, and they were two, three, and four stories tall, with neat green lawns and plenty of oleanders, hibiscus, and palm trees all around. I'd heard that before the developers would allow you to fork over $200,000 for a lot, you had to sign a pledge stating that you'd plant at least four palm trees. The oleanders and hibiscus, on the other hand, were optional.

When we turned off Stewart Road toward the development, there was a startlingly green golf course on our left where a couple of golfers from the development stood beside a red-and-white golf cart and wiped their foreheads while they swigged some kind of designer water from plastic bottles. On our right there was a small ranch with cattle grazing under oak trees in an open pasture.

"You'd think the ranch owners would just sell out," Dino said. "The way cattle prices are right now, they could make a lot more money by selling their land than they can from raising cows."

"They could make a lot more money by selling out even if cattle prices doubled," I said. "Or tripled. Maybe they just like working with cattle better than playing golf."

Dino grinned. "Yeah."

He liked money, but he didn't like golf. You had to play it outside. Of course, you had to go outside to take care of cattle, too, but if Dino owned a ranch he could hire someone to do all the work. He could probably have hired someone to play golf for him, too, but it wouldn't have been the same.

We turned left into the development, and I could see all the Jaguars parked beneath the houses. Lexus, Infiniti, and

Mercedes were well represented, though BMW didn't seem as popular as it once had. There was even a Cadillac or two.

I didn't see any other 1981 Pontiac Bonnevilles.

Canals leading to the bay ran beside most of the houses, and there were boats pulled up in slings, ready to drop down in the water at a moment's notice whenever the owner wanted a short cruise.

Garrison's house was on the bay side of the Island, which I assumed was his one concession to being a native. A lot of real Galvestonians pride themselves on how seldom they actually see the Gulf. The house was located right on the bay front so that there wouldn't be anything between it and the sunset.

It was pretty impressive, very modernistic, with shadows hiding in the sharp angles and the sun glinting off what seemed like acres of glass. Not to mention palm trees. There were a lot more than four. I counted ten before I stopped. No hibiscus, though.

The house sat on two lots instead of one, and figuring that construction costs ran somewhere in the neighborhood of two hundred dollars a square foot, we were looking at a house that had cost Lance about six hundred thousand bucks. Throw in the cost of the lots, and Garrison had spent something like a cool million on his little bait camp. That was quite a bit to a guy like me, but not much more than everyone else around him had laid out. I wondered if any of them had ever considered the risks.

Of course the Jags and other luxury cars would no doubt be somewhere inland if a hurricane blew across the island, but I thought it was a little foolish to spend six hundred grand for a house that could be toppled in seconds by a Force 2 gale. The stilts might keep the carpet dry when the storm surge came, but not if the house was already sinking into the bay. I wondered if the insurance carriers ever spent any sleepless nights thinking about what even a moderate storm could do. Probably not.

There were a black Acura Legend and a red Toyota MR-3 parked under Lance's house. Dino pulled in behind the Acura and said, "This is the place."

"You come here often?"

He gave me a look. "I asked for directions when Lance called me. I might not get out much, but I can follow directions."

"Getting a little touchy, are we?"

Dino didn't answer. He got out of the car and slammed the door behind him.

I got out, too, and stood there in the declining afternoon. The only sounds were from a power mower a couple of houses away and a couple of gulls circling overhead. Across the bay, the sun was beginning to sink. With the clouds over in that direction shading from gray to indigo, we were in for a spectacular sunset. I took a deep breath of the Gulf air, inhaling the scent of dead crabs, drying seaweed, salt, and sand.

"You gonna stand there and stare around, or are we going in?" Dino asked.

"What? You don't like it out here?"

He didn't have anything to say about that, either. He started up the stairway on the shady side of the house, and I followed along behind him.

"How long has it been since you saw Garrison?" I asked.

Dino stopped and turned back to look at me. "Nine or ten years, I guess. I do my business on the phone when I can. Why?"

"I just wondered if he was still 'Most Handsome.' "

"He never would've got that if the class had voted after you broke his nose."

"You think he remembers that?"

"I do," Dino said. "And you do. And it wasn't us who got our noses broken."

"So you're telling me you think he remembers?"

"I'm just saying that *I* remember. I don't know about Lance. Anyway, even if he remembers, he wants to see you. He asked me to bring you as a favor, so I'm bringing you. Are you getting cold feet?"

I wasn't, but I wasn't exactly eager to see Lance, either. He, Dino, and I had played on the high school football team together a long time ago, and Lance had had as much talent and ability as either of us, which, not to be overly modest about it, was saying a lot; Dino and I were both pretty good.

But Lance, who was wide receiver, dogged it on the field during practice, and he sometimes dogged it during a game. He was always worried that he might get hurt if he went all out, and there was a rumor that he was worried about more than getting hurt—he was afraid that he might get hit in the face and mess up his looks.

I'd confronted him in the dressing room after one particularly close game in which I'd thought he'd cost us a touchdown, and not so incidentally a win, because he'd chosen to fall down rather than try to run over a free safety whom he outweighed by twenty pounds.

I don't remember what I said, or what he answered, but I know that we were both suddenly angry in the way that seventeen-year-olds sometimes get angry, our faces red and the adrenaline surging through us like electric shocks.

He hit me first, though he later claimed that he hadn't. It didn't do him any good to make the claim, since everyone on the team was watching and saw him swing a looping right that slid off my cheekbone and opened a thin red cut.

I didn't wait for him to swing again. I punched him with a straight right to the nose and felt the satisfying crunch of cartilage giving way.

He hit the floor like he'd hit the field avoiding the safety, and that was the end of the fight. It was also the end of Lance

Garrison's football career. The trainer took him to the hospital, and he turned in his equipment the next Monday afternoon after the team had taken the field to practice. He never played another down.

I thought about my knee and how I'd ruined it later on in college. I would have been a lot smarter if I'd never played another down of football, either, but in those days I thought there was some kind of magic about me that would keep the injuries away forever.

I'd been wrong, of course.

"Well?" Dino said. "Are we going in, or are we going to stand out here on the stairs all day? You decide. It's you he wants to see."

"He didn't tell you why, huh?"

Dino gave an exaggerated sigh and looked up at the sky. The seagulls were still circling.

"Maybe he wants to break your nose," he said finally. "But it'll be dark in an hour or so. If we stay out here till then, we might be able to sneak away without him seeing us."

"Sarcasm doesn't become you," I said.

"Yeah. And neither does standing out here on the stairs all day."

"All right. Let's go see what Lance wants with me."

"Yeah," Dino said. "How bad can it be?"

"Probably no worse than a visit to the dentist," I said.

As it turned out in the long run, I was wrong about that, too.

3

LANCE CAME TO the door himself. I'd hoped that he'd look old and tired, that his face would have sagged and his hair fallen out.

Much to my disappointment, however, he looked pretty much the way he had in high school. There was a little gray in his hair, but there was still a lot of it. It was expensively cut, and most of it was still jet black, like his eyes. There were a few wrinkles in his forehead, but his chin still might have been chiseled from granite, and his mouth still had that little twist that was almost a sneer. He'd had his nose fixed; it was narrow and straight, and if I hadn't broken it myself, I would never have guessed that it had ever been less than perfect.

He was wearing Birkenstocks, a pair of tan cotton slacks with even fewer wrinkles than his face, and a navy blue sports shirt with no pockets. There was a colorful little polo player stitched on the left side of the shirt where a pocket should have been.

"Truman Smith," he said, sticking out his right hand. He was holding a drink of some kind in his left. "It's been a long time."

I think the proper response to that is supposed to be something like "Too long" or "You're right. It *has* been a long time. We should get together more often." But I didn't feel that way at all. As far as I was concerned, another twenty years or so wouldn't be too long, and I didn't want to get together with him now, much less more often.

So I shook his hand and said, "Hello, Lance. Dino says you want to talk to me about something."

He let go of my hand. "You always were direct, Tru. You, too, Dino. I haven't seen you for a while, either."

"I don't get out much," Dino said, and I laughed.

"What's so funny?" Lance asked, looking from Dino to me as if he thought we might be laughing at him.

"Private joke," I said.

"Oh," Lance said, smiling and showing his straight, white teeth. "Sure."

He led us through a short, paneled hall and into a long room fronted with heavily tinted glass. The hardwood floors gleamed where they weren't covered by what looked like genuine antique Persian rugs. I didn't have a good eye for that sort of thing, though. I bought my own rugs at one of K-Mart's remnant sales.

I looked up from the rugs and out over the bay at the sailboats tilting on the water and the clouds that were now beginning to turn reddish-orange around the edges as the sun sank behind them.

"Nice view," I said.

"That's why I built this place," Lance said. "You can't see a sunset like that in Houston."

"You can't even see the *sun* in Houston," Dino said. "Not most days, anyway."

Someone laughed, and I looked over to where a woman was sitting on a low couch that must have cost two or three times what Dino could get for his Pontiac.

I looked over and the woman smiled at me. "Hello, Tru. Dino hasn't changed a bit, has he?"

"Anne?" I said.

She laughed again. "I'm glad you recognized me. I was afraid I'd changed more than Dino has."

She hadn't changed at all, that was the thing. That was why my mouth was dry and why my knees were suddenly weak and why I felt as if a little man inside my chest was slugging me in the heart with a tiny sledgehammer.

"Close your mouth, Tru," Lance said. "Can I get you and Dino something to drink?"

"You got a Big Red?" Dino asked.

"A what?"

"Never mind. Bring me a gin and tonic and bring Tru here a glass of water. He looks like he needs it."

I needed something, that was for sure. "Water will be fine," I croaked.

"Perrier?"

"Tap water."

I didn't like water that fizzed, not unless it was flavored like Big Red. Lance shook his head at my unrefined tastes and disappeared from the room.

Anne got up from the couch and started toward me. Long legs in faded Levi's, blonde hair that fell to her shoulders. Blue eyes and red lips. I felt as awkward as if I were seventeen again.

When she got closer I could see the lines that crinkled the corners of her eyes and the way the blonde hair faded slightly to gray at the temples, but it didn't matter. She was still Anne Temple, the first girl I'd ever loved.

"It's been a long time, Tru," she said, extending her hand.

I took her hand, still smooth and slim, and this time I said what was expected. "Too long. If I'd known that you were in Galveston, I'd have tried to see you sooner."

"Oh, I don't live in Galveston. I just visit occasionally."

"Lance?" I had never regretted breaking his nose, and I found myself wanting to break it again.

"Sometimes. Sometimes I come to see my parents. They still live here. This time I came to see you."

"Me?"

"You can let go of her hand now," Dino said. "This isn't the senior prom."

I hadn't realized he was still in the room. I let Anne remove her hand from mine and said, "What did you want to see me about?"

"Lance will tell you. It's more his story than mine."

Lance came back into the room just then, carrying a silver tray with three glasses on it.

"And I'll tell you in a minute," he said, handing Dino a highball glass. "I believe you wanted water, Tru. I'm sorry I didn't have a jelly glass to put it in."

I took the water from the tray, drank most of it in one long swallow, and set the glass back on the tray that Lance was still holding. My throat didn't seem quite so dry now, and I looked at Anne again.

I hadn't seen her since our high school graduation. We'd broken up several months before that, in January or February, and I hadn't quite recovered by May. I think that what hurt me the most wasn't that she'd broken up with me but that she'd begun dating Lance.

She hadn't married him, though. I remembered that Jan, my sister, had sent me a clipping from the Galveston paper one year in my Christmas card. The clipping was an engagement photo of Anne, and the caption under the photo said that Anne was marrying the son of a rice farmer from somewhere around Eagle Lake. I didn't remember his name.

I'd kept the clipping for a couple of years and then thrown it away. I'd thought then that I was over Anne forever. Judging by the way I was feeling right now, that was another thing I'd been wrong about.

"Why don't we sit down and talk about old times?" Lance said.

I wasn't interested in old times at the moment, not unless Anne and I were alone. Then I might have a few things to say. But as far as Lance was concerned, I was doing a favor for Dino, and the favor didn't include reminiscing.

"I'd rather hear about what you wanted with me," I said. "And why you called Dino instead of me."

Lance shook his head. "Can we at least sit down?"

"Sure." I walked over to the couch where Anne had been. "Let's sit."

Lance came over, set the silver tray on a coffee table, and picked up his own drink. Anne and Dino trailed along behind him. I sat on the couch, hoping that Anne would sit beside me. She didn't. She sat in a wooden rocker. Dino and Lance sat beside me on the couch.

For a few seconds, we simply looked out through the glass at the clouds and the sailboats. Dino drank his gin and tonic, and Lance sipped at whatever it was that he had in his glass.

Finally Lance said, "I called Dino because I was afraid you wouldn't come if I called you. We weren't exactly best friends in high school."

He had a point. I probably wouldn't have come if he'd called me, not unless he'd mentioned that Anne would be there.

"Anyway," he said, "I've read a few things about you in the papers, and I knew that you and Dino were still friendly. Dino and I have been doing business for a long time, so I thought he might talk to you for me. I've made him more money than his uncles ever did."

At one time, back in the days when Galveston had been wide open, with gambling, prostitution, and just about any other illegal enterprise you could think of, Dino's uncles had run every racket on the Island. Times had changed. The uncles were gone, and everything was strictly legitimate now, or as legitimate as things ever were anywhere, but a lot of people on the Island remembered the uncles and the old days, usually with a great deal of affection and not a little regret.

"OK," I said. "Dino got me here. Since, as you say, we weren't the best of friends, you must want me for something pretty important."

Lance stretched his legs out in front of him and crossed his ankles. "Not really. But your name came up, so I thought I'd give you a try."

"My name came up?"

"My father-in-law asked for you," Anne said.

"Oh," I said. So that's why she was here to see me. Because of her father-in-law. I'd been sort of hoping that she might ask me to run away to Tahiti with her. Still, if what Lance wanted had to do with Anne, I might actually try to help him out.

But not if he wanted me to find someone.

"Her father-in-law is Red Lindeman," Lance said. "He works for me."

The name Lindeman jarred my memory, and I remembered that Anne had married a Paul Lindeman, but I'd never met either him or his father.

"What kind of work does Lindeman do?" I asked Lance, thinking about rice farming.

"He manages some ranch land I own."

I didn't know any more about ranch land or ranching than I knew about rice farms. "I've never heard of him. Where's this ranch land?"

"In the Eagle Lake area. You might never have heard of Red, but he's heard of you. He knows an old friend of yours."

"Oh? Who?"

"Fred Benton."

I'd done a little work for Fred not so long ago. "Fred told Lindeman about me? Why?"

It was Anne who answered. "He told him how you solved the murder of his alligator."

I looked over at her. "Has somebody murdered another one?"

"No," she said. She smiled, and the little guy with the sledge hit me another shot in the heart. "Not an alligator, not this time."

"What then?"

"A bird," Lance said. "This time, somebody killed a bird."

4

"A BIRD?" I don't know what I'd been expecting, but it sure hadn't been this. "Somebody killed a bird?"

"Not just any bird," Lance said. "It was an Attwater's prairie chicken."

"Thanks for clearing that up."

I was beginning to wonder if this whole thing was some kind of elaborate joke. Prairie chickens? I glanced at Dino, who was taking a drink of his gin and tonic.

He took the glass away from his mouth and swallowed. "Don't look at me. I'm just the go-between. I wouldn't know a prairie chicken from a goose."

"I'm not surprised," Lance said. "Hardly anyone knows about prairie chickens, these days. Why don't you tell them a little bit, Anne."

"All right. They're not really chickens, though."

Great. Someone had killed a chicken that wasn't really a chicken. I felt as if I'd wandered into a sequel to *Ace Ventura, Pet Detective*.

"If they aren't chickens, what are they?" I asked.

"They're actually grouse. They're just called chickens. I don't know why."

It probably didn't matter, anyway. A grouse by any other name.

"OK, you've got a dead grouse on your hands. Why do you care that one got killed?"

"Because there aren't many of them left," Anne said. "How many, Lance?"

"Sixty-eight, in the wild. That's the count for this year, anyway. There are maybe forty or fifty more in captivity."

"A hundred and eight or so in the whole world?" I said, wondering what difference it made.

"Prairie chickens are what you might call a *very* endangered species," Lance said. "There were a hundred and fifty-six in the wild at the previous count, so there was a considerable drop-off this year. There used to be even more, a lot more. A hundred years ago there were probably a million or so roaming around the coastal prairie."

"So what happened to them?"

"Lots of things," Anne said. "Hunters, for one. But the main reason they're disappearing is that the habitat's vanishing faster than they are. With all the development along the coast, there's no prairie anymore. It's not just the prairie chickens that are displaced, either. The snow geese have lost a lot of their habitat, too, and now they're nesting around the prairie chickens that are left. Some of the parasites from the geese have killed the prairie chickens."

I thought about the house we were sitting in, and all the others like it up and down the coast. And of the highways and industries and all the ever expanding cities and towns. No wonder the habitat was vanishing.

Lance must have read my mind. He said, "I'm not a developer. I just happen to own a house here. If I hadn't built here, someone else would have."

He was right, of course, but there seemed to be a little tinge of guilt in his words. Hearing it gave me more satisfaction than it should have.

"I'm not interested in your house or where it is," I told him. "But I would like to know what this dead bird has to do with your ranch land. Or with me."

"Here's what it has to do with my land. I entered into a deal with the federal government. They put some prairie chickens on my land and managed them for three years. They improved the land, got rid of some of the brush, and created a habitat for the birds. They turned things over to me this year, and I turned them over to Red Lindeman. He sees to things like mowing and controlling the pests and predators. We have to be very careful, and we are. But now, one of the birds is dead."

"And Lindeman wants me to do something about it?"

"That's right. He wants you to investigate. I know it sounds crazy, but he knows Fred Benton, and Benton told him all about that business with the alligator. Red already knew part of it, read about it in the paper. That's why he talked to Fred in the first place."

"But we're talking about an endangered species," I said. "The government will send in all the investigators you want."

Lance shook his head. "They've already sent in someone, and that's one more than Red wants. He doesn't like the man, and he doesn't think he's competent. He wants you."

"What do you have to do with all this?" I asked Anne. I didn't care about Lindeman or Garrison, and I didn't care much about prairie chickens, but I cared about her.

"I'm interested in the birds," she said. "And maybe I feel a little guilty. Red is my father-in-law, and he was a rice farmer for a long time. He killed his share of birds of one kind or another over the years."

A lot of the rice farmers had put out poison until the

government stopped them. The farmers had a pretty good argument for what they'd done. They were trying to make a living, and birds of all kinds were eating their crops. But the farmers couldn't use the poison anymore.

"What about your husband?" I asked. "Does he still farm?"

"Paul? No. He works for Lance."

"Doing what?"

"He manages my radio station," Lance said. "KLWG."

Lance's full name was Lance Wayne Garrison. I was glad to learn that he was just as modest as he'd always been.

"Where is this radio station of yours?"

"In Picketville. It's the only station there."

I would have laid odds on that. Picketville, not far from Eagle Lake, was hardly big enough to support one radio station, much less any others.

"We have a pretty good-sized listening audience," Lance said, reading my mind again. "We carry talk shows all day and all night. People like talk radio these days."

"Most talk-show hosts I've heard aren't into saving prairie chickens," I said.

Lance laughed. "Not hardly. But I don't endorse the shows or the hosts. I just put them on the air and bank the money the sponsors pay me for the airtime. You know what the canned announcements say: 'The views expressed on the shows heard on KLWG do not necessarily reflect those of the station's owner.' Or words to that effect."

"Plausible deniability," I said.

"What's that supposed to mean?"

"Nothing. Just a phrase I heard one time."

Lance's face darkened. "Look, Smith, we never got along very well, and I didn't really want to deal with you on this. But Red's being stubborn, so I thought I'd give it a shot. I gave it one, but I don't think it's going to work out. Maybe we'd better just call it off and let you get back to whatever it is that you do."

"Background checks," I said.

"I—what?"

"Background checks. That's what I do."

He didn't seem impressed, not that I blamed him. I'd tried my hand at a couple of jobs since coming back to Galveston. I'd painted houses for a while, and until recently I'd been working for a bail bondsman, a job I'd left mainly because I didn't get along very well with the boss.

Background checking was something that I could do at home. All I needed was a computer, the right software, and a modem. People don't realize how much information about them is available these days, and it's available to just about anyone. For example, if you know nothing more than someone's date of birth and first name, you can dial up a place near Dallas and get the someone's last known address.

Credit checks are even easier, and if you're stumped on something, private eyes all over the country are on-line. All you have to do is ask for their help and advice. They're usually glad to give it.

And if I needed any illegal hacking done, I could always call on my friend Johnny Bates. He claims that he can get into any computer system that he wants to get into, up to and including the one in the Department of Defense, and I don't have any reason to doubt him.

And, of course, if worse comes to worst, there's always the telephone. You can get the phone numbers of nearly every telephone subscriber in the country on CD-ROM.

"Whose backgrounds do you check?" Lance asked.

"Anyone's. But mostly I work for women who want to know something about the men they're dating or thinking about marrying. There's a shocking lack of trust these days."

I'd even been shocked myself at the response I got to the

two small ads I'd placed in a couple of big-city newspapers. It had taken me less than a month to become comfortably established in my new line of work.

Of course, considering some of the things I found out about prospective fiancés and lovers, it was no surprise that there was such a lack of trust. The number of lies I uncovered amazed even me, not to mention the women I was working for.

"I'll bet it's really lucrative, too," Lance said. "But I was thinking of paying you five hundred dollars a day."

"Plus expenses," I said.

"Of course. I thought that went without saying."

"I'll look into your bird caper, then," I said.

Lance smiled his slightly sneery smile. "I thought you might."

It wasn't the money, though I didn't bother to disturb Lance's smile by telling him that. He wouldn't have believed me anyway, so let him think whatever he pleased.

"You'll have to run over to Picketville and talk to Red," he said. "I think Red's blowing this way out of proportion, but I suppose you'll have to do some investigating. You do remember how to investigate?"

"I think so. You check out Colonel Mustard and make sure he doesn't have the lead pipe hidden in his jock."

For some reason Lance didn't think that was funny. "It won't be that easy. But I think it's more than likely that somebody shot the bird by accident. Red doesn't agree with me, though."

"Did he say why?"

"I'll let him tell you that," Lance said. "I don't want to prejudice you. You'll probably have to stay in Picketville for a day or so to satisfy Red that you're at least trying. Check into the Picketville Inn and tell the clerk you're working for me. He'll comp you; I own the place."

"Sure," I said. I didn't mind if he wanted to save a few bucks on my accommodations.

"When can you start?" he asked.

I glanced over at Anne, who had turned her attention to the sunset. The clouds were a deep, dark purple now, and the sun was sinking low behind them, making the higher clouds glow orange and pink. I couldn't see the sailboats anymore.

I sat quietly and looked out the window for a few seconds, then asked Anne, "When are you going back?"

"Tonight," she said.

I smiled. "Then that's when I can start."

5

ON THE DRIVE back to my house, Dino made it clear that he thought I was crazy.

"It's a dead chicken, for Christ's sake," he said. "You're gonna investigate a dead chicken."

The Pontiac's radio was tuned to a Houston oldies station, and Roy Orbison was belting out "Only the Lonely." Now and then the clouds would move aside and uncover the full moon. I was sure that if I tried, I could come close to remembering how I'd felt on nights like that twenty years ago.

"It's not a chicken," I said. "It's a grouse."

"Like that makes a difference. Chicken, grouse, it's still some damn dead bird. You're gonna try to find out who killed a bird."

"And make five hundred dollars a day," I reminded him. "Don't forget that. Not to mention expenses."

"Yeah, that's why you're going, all right. I'm sure Anne doesn't have a thing to do with it."

"She's married," I said. "What could she have to do with my going?"

"She's pretty friendly with Lance, for a married lady."

"They're just old friends. They knew each other when they were kids."

"Right."

"You always did have a dirty mind, Dino. You can't make anything out of Anne visiting an old friend from high school."

"I guess not. She visits me all the time. And you, too, probably. We just forgot to mention it when we were talking about things."

"She hasn't visited me, but maybe she didn't know I was here."

"Gimme a break."

"All right. Let's just forget it." I didn't want to talk about it anymore, but Dino wasn't going to let it drop.

"What's Cathy gonna think if you go running off to see Anne?" he asked.

Cathy Macklin was the woman I'd been going with for a while. I didn't want to talk about her, either.

"She'll think I'm going to do a job," I said. "Anne doesn't have anything to do with it."

Dino snorted disgustedly. "Sure. I forgot. It's the five hundred dollars a day."

Roy Orbison had been replaced by the Beatles singing "All My Lovin'."

"Five hundred dollars a day is more than I'm making by doing background checks," I said. "Besides, I need to get out of the house and off the Island more. It wouldn't hurt you to do the same thing. You want to come with me?"

"Somebody has to stay here and feed the cat. You didn't forget about the cat, did you?"

To tell the truth, I had forgotten about the cat, a sure sign that I wasn't thinking clearly.

"OK," I said. "You're right. I'm going because of Anne.

But it's not like you think. I'm just glad to be able to do her a favor."

"Sure you are. And you're such good buddies with Lance that you can't resist helping him out."

Sometimes I wish Dino didn't know me so well. I decided that I might as well tell the truth, or come as close to telling it as I could. I wasn't entirely sure how I really felt about things.

"Seeing Anne after all this time gave me a pretty good shock," I admitted.

"Now there's a news flash," Dino said. "If your jaw had been hanging any lower, you'd have stepped on it."

"That obvious, huh?"

"Even Lance noticed. What does that tell you?"

It told me that my surprise had been obvious to everyone. Lance had never been known for his sensitivity to the feelings of anyone other than himself.

"Do you think people ever really change?" I asked as Dino pulled off onto the oyster-shell drive leading to my house. "After high school, I mean."

"Sure they do. How much did you weigh when you graduated?"

"I don't mean physical changes, and you know it."

"Yeah. Well, Lance hasn't changed much. He's still an asshole. I couldn't say about Anne, but she didn't look like she was still madly in love with you, if that's what you mean."

"That's not what I mean," I said, though I wasn't sure that was true. "I mean Lance. You're right about him. Of course, he probably thinks the same thing about me."

"I wonder why," Dino said, stopping the Pontiac in front of the house.

"Dion and the Belmonts," I said. "1958."

"Huh?"

"Never mind. You want to come in the house? It's your house, after all. We could have something to eat."

Dino looked at the house. "You actually have something to eat?"

He had me there.

"No," I admitted. "Not unless you like peanut butter."

"Peanut butter's OK, but I've got a better idea. Why don't you pack your bag and say good-bye to the cat. Then we'll go somewhere and eat. My treat."

That sounded like a good idea to me. It didn't take me long to pack. I just threw *Tobacco Road*, a shaving kit, a few pairs of jeans, and short-sleeved sweatshirts into a black nylon sports bag. I don't dress up a lot.

The only tough decision I had to make was whether to take my pistol or not. I didn't think the murder of a prairie chicken was serious enough to warrant the heavy artillery, so I left the pistol in its zippered case in the closet.

"Where's the cat?" Dino asked when I came back into the living room carrying my bag.

"Out tormenting geckos, probably. I'll leave him a bowl of Tender Vittles on the porch by his water. You can check on him in the morning."

Dino looked at me.

"If you don't mind," I said. "I wouldn't want to put you out."

Dino stood up. "Sure you wouldn't. But I don't mind. That cat's beginning to succumb to my charms. By the time you get back, he might even have moved in with me."

"That might not be a bad idea. You could use the company."

"Yeah. You planning to call Cathy?"

"As soon as we decide where to eat."

"Mexican food. You can meet me at the restaurant after you make the call and feed your cat."

He went outside to his car, and I went to the telephone.

WE ATE AT The Original Mexican Restaurant, not far from The Strand. We had fajitas for two. I thought that Dino ate more than his share, but I didn't mention it to him. After all, he was paying.

When we left the restaurant, Dino said, "Don't get yourself into more trouble than you can handle."

"Like you said, it's only a chicken."

"Grouse."

"Whatever."

"Yeah. But that's not what I mean, and you know it."

"Don't worry about me and Anne. I know that whatever there was between us was over a long time ago. We were just kids, after all."

"You still remember it, though, the way Lance remembers that broken nose. You might not want to talk about it, but you remember. What did Cathy say?"

"About what?"

"About Anne."

"I don't think I mentioned her."

"What *did* you mention, aside from the five hundred bucks a day?"

"I think I mentioned something about doing my part to prevent the disappearance from the earth of a species vital to the survival of humanity."

"Jesus, Tru."

"You think I laid it on a little thick?"

Dino shook his head. "Oh, no. Hell, no. I'd have done the same thing in your position."

"What position is that?"

"The position of a guy who's sneaking out of town to see an old girlfriend in the hope that she's still got fond memories of the way things were a long time ago."

"You've got it all wrong," I said.

Maybe he did, and maybe he didn't. I wasn't even sure myself.

"I may be wrong," he said, "but I saw the look on your face when you saw her this afternoon."

"She took me by surprise. I know you can't recapture the past."

"You remember that book everybody has to read in college, the one about the guy with the big yellow car? He was always standing on the end of his dock looking at some green light."

I hadn't realized Dino was so literary. "You mean *The Great Gatsby*?"

"That's the one. You remember what happened to him?"

"Who?"

"Who are we talking about here? Gatsby, that's who."

"I remember."

"Well, keep it in mind."

I said that I would, and clapped him on the shoulder.

He was still standing on the sidewalk watching me when I drove away.

6

I WAS DRIVING a little blue-and-white Chevy S-10 pickup that I'd bought a few months ago. I got the money for it by selling the Jeep that Fred Benton had given me after I'd found out who killed his alligator.

Fred said at the time that it was an authentic World War II–mode Jeep, but I'd never really believed him. Then one day a guy flagged me down on the street. He was vacationing in Galveston, and he was an automobile collector. He wanted to know how much I'd take for my Jeep.

After I did a little checking into prices for genuine antique Jeeps and after a little haggling, the collector and I arrived at a price that was satisfactory to both of us, especially to me. I was glad to get the money because it allowed me to buy a nifty home computer with a modem. That was all I needed to set up my background-checking business and quit my job with the bail bondsman.

The truck was just a bonus. It wasn't new, but it had an AM/FM radio and air-conditioning. Its biggest advantage over the Jeep, however, was that it had a roof for when it rained, which was fairly often if you lived on Galveston Island.

I drove up Highway 6 through Hitchcock and Santa Fe. At Alvin, I turned off 6 and got on a farm road that led to Highway 36. Once I got to 36, I turned right and went up to Rosenberg. I went through the edge of town, past the K-Mart Super Store, and then headed west.

The clouds were ragged here, not as thick as they had been over the Island, and the full moon had risen, high and bright. It made my headlights almost unnecessary. The road in front of me stretched out like a dark ribbon, and the fields to my left and right were bathed in the pale light, with moon shadows chasing across them.

The road was straight and the land was flat. There were no trees and hardly any houses, just seemingly endless fields of rice and grain, with a little cotton mixed in, and I was the only one on the road.

I was running along with the windows down, enjoying the air that was not quite as humid as that on the Island and that had no smell of salt in it, and thinking about the times when Anne and I had driven down Seawall Boulevard with the night wind coming in off the Gulf and smelling like all the faraway places we thought we'd see some day.

I'd never seen them. Maybe Anne had. Maybe I'd see her in Picketville. Maybe she'd tell me about them.

That was a lot of "maybes" and they made me wonder what Anne had been doing all those years that I hadn't seen her. They made me wonder if she'd ever thought of me in all that time.

While wallowing in my nostalgic mood, I was listening to the same oldies station that Dino had tuned his radio to, but in the middle of Buddy Holly singing "Rave On," I passed a sign that said TURN YOUR DIAL TO KLWG AM FOR TALK THAT MAKES UNCOMMON SENSE.

There was a frequency given, one that was far to the right on the dial. Feeling a little stupid for obeying a sign, I switched off Buddy Holly and changed to the AM setting, then tuned the knob to KLWG.

I was just in time for the closing message on "The Reverend Clyde Callahan's Full Gospel Worship Hour." The message consisted mostly of a strong suggestion, if not an outright plea, that the Reverend Clyde's listeners send as much money as they possibly could to the address that the good reverend kept repeating over and over.

I figured that KLWG was mostly preachers at night, and I wasn't in the mood for a sermon. I was about to change the station when I heard the opening notes of "The Stars and Stripes Forever." I'm a sucker for Sousa, so I dropped my hand and listened.

As the strains of the march faded, a deep voice came on the air. It wasn't a cultured voice, and it wasn't a trained voice. It wasn't even an educated voice. But it had one important quality: It sounded good on the radio, smooth and sincere. There was a hint of an East Texas accent that might grate a bit on the ears of someone born north of, say, Oklahoma, but nothing that would bother anyone likely to be listening to KLWG. The speaker identified himself as Ralph Evans and said that he'd be taking calls from the listeners in a little while. But first he had a few things to say.

"What I want to talk about is the New World Order. Y'all know about it. It's no big secret."

It might not be a secret to Ralph Evans's regular listeners, but I didn't know about it. I turned up the volume a little so I could hear better over the noise of the air rushing by.

"Yessir," Ralph Evans said, "the United States government, the one that pretends to represent you and me up there in Washington, D.C., would like for all of us in this country to be a part of the New World Order, right in there with China and Russia and a lot of other godless places like that. One big world government, that's what they want. And you all know what your part would be in something like that."

Evans paused, as if waiting for his invisible audience to answer. I would have answered, but I didn't know what to say.

Apparently I was the only one, because Evans said, "That's right! Diddly-squat. That's what your part would be. They're gonna take away your car and your land and your house and make it all a part of their big socialist scheme."

Evans paused again, and all I could hear was the air and the hum of my tires on the highway.

"But you think you're not gonna let that happen, don't you? You think you've got your guns cleaned and oiled and your places all picked out where you can make a stand. You think you know what's comin' down the road, and you think you can do something about it. Well, I'm here to tell you, friends, you're as wrong as you can be about that."

There was a second of silence, and I could imagine Evans shaking his head sadly as he looked at his microphone.

"You're wrong," he went on, "because you don't know the whole story. Sure, you know all about how they want to take away your guns and even your right to own guns. And if they can't do that, they durn sure want to make sure you register every one you got so they can come and get it in the dark of night. You know all that.

"But what you don't know is what I've just had reported to me today. It comes from a good source, one that I trust and one that's had good information before. It's the one that told me about the leftover leg in the Murrah Federal Building up there in Oklahoma City, the leg the government didn't want you to know about and never would've told you about if it hadn't been for broadcasters like me, people who aren't afraid to tell the stories the left-wing-dominated media won't tell you, people who want to keep this country free and out of the hands of the one worlders up there in Washington.

"What I'm sayin' is that this is a source we can trust. And what he tells me is that right now, even while I'm talkin' to you on the radio here, *right now, this very minute*, the so-called government of the people is buildin' concentration camps right here in Texas!

"Where are they? Out in West Texas, out in that godforsaken Big Bend area, out there where you can drive for about a day and a half and not see anything except a goat and a rock, that's where. I can't give you the exact location over the air, but if you call in to the station and talk to old Larry, who's workin' the phones tonight, he'll tell you. He's got the coordinates.

"And what are these concentration camps for? Now that's the scary part, folks, because those camps are for you and me. That's right. You and me, people who believe that we not only have a right to keep and bear arms but who actually have weapons in our homes. We're the ones they're afraid of. We're the ones they're after.

"They've got our names down in their book if we've ever registered one of our weapons. They know where we live, and they know they can come after us when we least expect 'em. If you don't think they can, ask Mr. Randy Weaver. Or ask Mr. David Koresh."

There was another pause. The Chevy's tires hummed and the air rushed by.

"On second thought, I don't guess you can ask Mr. Koresh, can you? You-all know what happened to him. You don't need me to repeat it for you.

"And it can happen to you if you don't go along peacefully when they ring your doorbell in the dead of night and ask you to come quietly so they can put you in one of their camps and use you for slave labor for the rest of your life. You and your wife and your kids, too, believe me. Unless they take them off somewhere for breeding stock. They might stoop to that, too. They've done just about everything else.

"I know you're shocked. I know you're surprised. Even with everything else the government's done to you, this is hard for you to believe. But it's the truth, every last word of it, and I'm gonna take your calls about it right after you listen to these messages."

"The Stars and Stripes Forever" faded in again, and then there was a commercial for Bud's Surplus Store, followed by one for Wadle's Feed and Seed. The one after that was for a car dealer in Houston.

After that, people started calling in. The first caller, Mike, who didn't give his last name and didn't want to say where he lived so as not to make it any easier for the feds to find him, said that Ralph was one hundred percent correct about the concentration camps. Mike had already heard about them from a buddy who was as trustworthy as Ralph's own source.

"He's seen those big black DOD helicopters flyin' around out there in West Texas," Mike said, "but when you ask about 'em, you don't get any answers. We know what they're for, though. They're keepin' watch over the area to make sure nobody gets in. And later on, after those camps are finished, they'll make just as sure nobody gets out."

"So what are we gonna do, Mike?" Ralph asked. "Are we gonna just sit idly by and let them come in and take us right out of our houses and put us in the humvees and haul us off to the camp?"

"Hell, no," Mike said. "You know better than that, Ralph. I'm ready for the bastards. I've got my guns, and I've bought me some of those frangible rounds, and I've tried 'em out. Let me tell you somethin', boy, those suckers will get the job done."

"I just bet they will, but aren't they pretty expensive, Mike?"

"Hell, what does that matter when it's your future at stake, Ralph? Sure, some of 'em go for maybe four bucks a round, but there's some for about two-fifty, and even those'll put a four-and-a-half-inch hole in anybody that walks."

"The question is," Ralph said, "how do they work against bullet-proof vests? They'll all be wearing vests when they come for you, Mike."

"Head shot," Mike said. "Either that or go for the groin area. The way those frangible rounds tear you up, you sure wouldn't want to be shot in the groin."

I didn't know about anyone else who was listening, but I didn't want to be shot in the groin with anything, frangible or not. I wondered how Evans would follow up on Mike's idea, but it was time for more messages from the sponsors. This time the first message was a gag commercial for "the essential emergency ration for every survivalist's backpack," something called "Spotted Owl in a Can." At least I think it was a gag.

When Evans came back, Mike was gone and someone named Tom was on the line. Tom wanted to talk about how to convert his AR-15 to full-automatic, but Ralph said they didn't talk about things like that over the air. There was, however, a book he could recommend.

I listened to the program for another half hour as I headed toward Picketville, and the more I heard, the more I realized how important it was for Lance to dissociate himself from the views expressed by some of the hosts on his station. I suspected that at least some of Lance's friends might have been a little put off by Ralph Evans, though I might have been wrong. I didn't know any of Lance's friends.

I didn't want to know any of them, either, other than Anne. Lance's friends didn't concern me, and neither did his radio station. When I pulled into the parking lot of the Picketville Inn, I turned off the radio. I was there to find out who killed a prairie chicken, not to worry about Lance Garrison.

7

PICKETVILLE WAS A little town that was a long way
from anywhere. It had been founded by cotton farmers, but
now the gin was deserted, not much more than a home for rats
and spiders; there wasn't enough cotton grown in the area to
justify keeping it in operation. There was, however, a grain
elevator about the size of the Trump Tower standing by the
railroad tracks a half mile from town, making it clear what
the economic mainstay of the area was.

The highway ran right through the center of town and
became its main street. I drove past Wadle's Feed and Seed
just before I came to the city limits sign, and Bud's Surplus
Store was just a little farther along. After going by Bud's, I
passed a hardware store, a barbershop, a jewelry store, two
department stores, a furniture store, two drugstores, a video
rental shop, a couple of fried chicken and hamburger stands,
a restaurant, and two supermarkets, along with a couple of
convenience stores that sold everything from gasoline to gro-
ceries. After that I was out of town, and the road bent back to
the left in a long curve.

The Picketville Inn was just around the curve, a genuine relic of the 1950s, when it had probably been called a tourist court. There were ten or twelve separate stuccoed buildings, each one an individual unit, and they all glowed a uniform shade of pale green in the light shed by the giant neon sign sitting high on a pole in front of the office, a building only a little larger than the others.

The sign said that this was the Picketville Inn and that there was a vacancy. I wasn't surprised. I hadn't seen anything in the vicinity that looked like a major tourist attraction, not unless you were into grain elevators.

I saw only two cars at the Inn. One was parked in front of one of the units and one was at the office. The one at the office was an old Ford with a bumper sticker that said My Safety's Off, Ralph, an obvious reference to what I assumed to be one of Ralph Evans's tag lines: "When they knock on your door, be sure your safety's off." He'd repeated it several times while I was listening to his show.

I parked near the office and got out of the Chevy, stretching my legs and back. When I opened the office door, I could hear a radio tuned to KLWG. Ralph Evans was still holding forth.

The night clerk was a young man not more than twenty-five. He was resting his elbows on the counter and reading a magazine. He didn't seem to be paying any attention to the radio. His complexion was bad, and a toothpick jutted from the corner of his mouth. He was wearing a camo cap and a T-shirt that had a slogan on it. I couldn't read the slogan.

He looked up from the magazine and said, "He'p you?"

"I'd like to check in," I said. "My name is Truman Smith; I'm working for Lance Garrison."

He straightened up and I could read the words printed on his T-shirt: FEAR THE GOVERNMENT THAT FEARS YOUR GUNS.

The toothpick jiggled and he said, "Oh. Yeah. He called

and said you'd be comin' in. You can take Number Two, second on the right."

He reached under the counter and brought out a heavy brass key and plastic tag attached to a silver chain. He plunked the key down on the counter.

"There ya go," he said, and looked back down at his magazine.

I picked up the key, tossed it in the air, and caught it in my right hand. The old reflexes were still in great shape.

"Don't I have to sign anything?" I asked, closing my fingers over the key.

He didn't look up. "Nah. It's all taken care of."

Apparently the management of the Picketville Inn took a pretty casual approach to the formalities. That was fine with me. I went out and got in the truck. Number 2 wasn't far, but each unit had a separate covered parking place. I figured I might as well take advantage of it.

I parked the truck and unlocked the door to my room. There was a light switch to the left of the door, and I flipped it up. There was a ceiling light, something you don't see in many motels these days, and the furniture was as obsolete as the motel itself. There was a real bed, not just a headboard attached to the wall with a bed frame extending out from it, and the dresser, table, and chairs were solid wood. Everything was a little worn and scratched, and the rug was as thin as an old man's undershirt. The only modern furnishings in the room were the clock radio on the end table and the TV set on the dresser. Even the telephone was a solid black desk model with a dial. I hadn't seen one like it in years.

I threw my bag in the middle of the bed. It was too late to call Red Lindeman, but I thought Anne might call me. She knew I'd be here.

I unzipped the bag and took out *Tobacco Road*. Then I

plumped up the pillows on the bed, put them behind my back, and started reading.

An hour passed and no one had called. I realized that I'd been indulging in a silly little romantic fantasy. I hadn't seen Anne for a very long time, and there was no reason to think that she had been especially glad to see me when we'd met at Lance's. She apparently visited Lance every so often, but she'd never made an attempt to get in touch with me.

And she was married, probably very happily. I'd be seeing her in the course of finding out what had happened to the prairie chicken, I supposed, but there was no reason to think my seeing her would lead to anything more. It wasn't going to be like some sentimental novel in which old sweethearts find each other after years apart and realize that they're destined to spend the rest of their lives together.

I read a few more pages in the novel and then went to bed.

I DREAMED ABOUT BIRDS.

I don't know what kind of birds I dreamed about. They certainly weren't prairie chickens, and they probably weren't real birds at all. They were black, and there were a lot of them, and they soared up out of a grain field, rising and falling in a dark cloud against a lead-colored sky.

I'm not especially fond of birds; on the whole, I like cats much better. I was glad when the dream ended.

THE NEXT MORNING I ate breakfast at the restaurant I'd passed in town. It was a blue building with THE TOOLE SHED painted on it in black letters. Under the name there was another line that said "Try Our Blue Plate Special or Our Famous Jalapeño Burger."

I decided that jalapeño burgers might be fine for some other time, but not so early in the morning.

The interior of the restaurant was filled with Formica-topped tables and booths upholstered with some kind of imitation leather. Antlers of all sizes hung from the walls and ceilings, and in the midst of them, on one wall, was a stuffed alligator. Near the door was a sign that said PLEASE SEAT YOURSELF.

There were plenty of customers, most of them men and most of them wearing gimme caps or straw cowboy hats. They were reading newspapers or talking in low tones. It was a small town, and everyone in the restaurant probably knew everyone else. As a stranger, I didn't create much of a stir. Several people looked up as I came in and then looked back at their food or their newspaper or whoever was sitting at the table with them.

I sat at one of the tables and took a menu from between a bottle of ketchup and the napkin holder. I could get two eggs, toast, bacon, and coffee for a buck and a half.

A woman came over to take my order. Her name tag said she was "Linda." She was slim and professional and looked more like a nurse than a waitress.

"Good morning," she said. "What can I get you?"

I gave her my order.

"How do you want those eggs?"

"Scrambled," I said.

"Whole wheat toast, or white?"

"Whole wheat." I might as well be healthy.

"Dry or buttered?"

"Dry." Healthier still.

"This is the first time I've waited on you. Next time you come in, I'll remember."

I believed her. She probably knew everyone in town, so I decided to test her.

"Do you know a man named Red Lindeman?" I asked.

"I know just about everybody in Picketville, honey," she said. "I've owned this place for twenty years, and everybody in town's eaten here, at least once in that time. Red comes in nearly every day."

"Is he here now?"

She looked over the crowd. "He sure is, honey." She tilted her head to her left. "He's sittin' right over there in that booth by the wall."

I looked over and saw a big man wearing an Astros cap and a blue cotton work shirt. He had a plate of poached eggs and sausage in front of him, and he was eating steadily.

"I think I'll join him," I said.

"Are you right sure about that, honey?"

"You can bring my eggs over there, can't you?"

"Sure enough. If you want to sit with Red, you go ahead and do it."

I pushed back my chair, but no one paid me much attention, not until I slid into the booth. Then it seemed to me that conversations all over the restaurant died down and all eyes turned to look in my direction for about half a second before sliding away.

Lindeman looked up from his sausage and eggs, but he didn't put down his fork. His weathered face was slightly freckled, and gray hair that still had a slight reddish tinge stuck out around the bottom of the cap.

"Who the hell are you?" he said.

"Truman Smith. Lance Garrison sent me."

He looked me over. "How do I know you're really Smith?"

I reached in my back pocket and pulled out my wallet. "Want to see my driver's license?"

"Hell, no."

I showed it to him anyway.

"Damn sorry picture," he said.

I agreed with him and slipped the wallet back into my pocket.

"You helped Fred Benton with that alligator business," he said.

I admitted that I had. "But I don't specialize in animals."

"Didn't figure you did. But I guess you don't mind helpin' with this one, you bein' a friend of Lance's and all."

"I wouldn't say we were friends."

"Don't matter. You know him."

I admitted that, too. Reluctantly. "Why don't you tell me about the prairie chicken?" I asked.

"Will when I finish my breakfast," he said. "Eggs are gettin' cold." He shoved a forkful of poached egg into his mouth.

Watching people chew food isn't one of my favorite ways to kill time, so I looked around the restaurant. No one was looking back.

Linda came with my food soon enough, and I dove in. My usual breakfast was a bowl of Cheerios, so I enjoyed the change.

Linda kept returning to fill my coffee cup. "You and Red gettin' along all right?" she asked on the third or fourth trip.

"Just fine," I said, and Red grunted.

"Red's not the most popular fella in town these days," Linda said. "Or did you notice?"

"I noticed," I told her.

"Thought you might've." She laid the check on the table and went away.

Red pushed his plate forward. "She thinks she knows ever'thing that goes on in this town."

"Does she?"

"Just about. Owns this place, been here a long time."

"Is she the one who named it?"

"Yeah, Linda Toole. The Toole Shed. Cute, huh?"

"If you like that sort of thing." I ate the last bite of my eggs and said, "Now what about that prairie chicken?"

"Let's get outta here," he said. "I'll tell you all about it on the way to Lance's place."

"All right," I said, and we slid out of the booth.

We were almost to the cash register when three men came through the front door. They didn't all come through at the same time; two of them were so big that they could barely get through it alone.

The first one through looked like a poster boy for steroids. He looked so hard that a sharp knife wouldn't penetrate any farther than his epidermis, and his face might have been hacked out of a block of wood. He was dressed in camo fatigues and wearing a camo cap. A ponytail not more than two inches long stuck out of the hole in the back of the cap. Maybe he was a Steven Seagal fan.

The man in the middle was just average size, and he was wearing a pair of baggy jeans, boots, and a Western shirt that was too tight on his pudgy body. His eyes were small and too close together, and he needed a shave.

The third man, while not as big as the first, looked meaner. His mouth was a thin slash and looked as if it had never smiled. He was wearing camos, and I thought that Bud's Surplus must do a booming business. He was one of the few men in The Toole Shed besides me without a cap. His hair was cut so close to his head that it was no longer than the stubble on the second man's chin.

The first man brushed by me, leaning in and jarring me slightly with his shoulder, a glancing blow that might have been an accident. I felt his upper arm as it brushed me; it was as hard as a bois d'arc block.

I looked at the man, and he smiled, showing me yellow teeth the size of fingernails.

I was fishing in the Gulf one day a year or so ago. There

was no chop on the water, just a gentle swell, and I had waded out beyond the second sandbar. I was far down the Island, away from the crowds. I hadn't caught any fish, but I was enjoying the day, the blue sky, the wheeling gulls, the breeze off the water.

And then I moved. Not much, just enough to change my position, and the sand beside my right foot boiled up through the green water and a wide, dark shadow slid off the floor of the Gulf.

A chill surged through me like an electric shock. I had missed stepping on the stingray by inches, and the thought of its paralyzing barb stabbing into my calf was almost enough to immobilize me.

There was something about the big man's manner and smile that affected me very much in the same way. There was the same dark threat in them, the same disinterested menace as in the stingray's proximity.

He didn't say he was sorry for bumping me, and I didn't ask him for an apology.

Red Lindeman ignored all three men and paid his check as if nothing had happened. I watched the men sit at a table and pick up the menus. I watched Linda Toole as she went over to wait on the table. Her mouth was turned down at the corners, and I didn't think she would call any of them "honey."

I paid the cashier and went through the door into the warm sunshine of the parking lot.

"Who were those guys?" I asked Lindeman, who was waiting for me outside the door.

"The one that bumped you was Gar Thornton, and the one in the back was Bert Ware. They're the bodyguards for the one in the middle. Ralph Evans."

"You know them?"

"Oh, yeah," he said. "I know 'em all right."

8

LINDEMAN MIGHT HAVE known the men, but they were something else he didn't want to talk about right then.

"We'll get to 'em sooner or later," he said. "Where's your car?"

I pointed at the Chevy. "Right over there."

"You can leave it there and ride with me. Won't anybody bother it."

He led me to a battered Dodge Ram. "Four-wheel drive," he said. "Sometimes you need that around here after a big rain."

I climbed in on the passenger side. "Where are we going?"

"Out to Garrison's place. That's where the dead bird is."

"You've still got it?"

He started the engine and the whole truck shook. "Put it in the deep freeze. That gover'ment fella tried to take it, but I wouldn't let him. He was about as useless as the tits on a boar hog. Tried to tell me that the shootin' was just an accident, when I know better. I was glad to see his taillights turn the corner."

"He's left town?"

Lindeman pulled the truck out onto the street without bothering to check the traffic. That was all right, I guess, since there wasn't any traffic.

" 'Left town' is right," he said. "What he said was that he'd 'wrapped up the investigation.' Said some hunter shot that bird by accident and that's all there was to it."

"But you know better."

"Damn sure do. What would a hunter be huntin' right about now?"

I didn't know the answer to that one, and said so.

"Well, at least you admit your ignorance, which is more than that gover'ment fella would do. The answer is, nothin'. There ain't no birds in season right now."

The Dodge rattled through town and headed in the direction of the Picketville Inn. In a few seconds we passed the Inn and kept right on going.

"People don't always stick to the season," I said.

"'Course not. But season or no season, you'd damn sure better not be huntin' birds on Garrison's place. Those birds are all protected by the government. Anyway, say you shot a bird by accident, what'd you do with it?"

I thought about that for a few seconds. "Get rid of it. Or maybe take it home and eat it if it was good for eating."

"Damn right. You wouldn't leave it on a fella's doorstep, now would you?"

"No. Is that what happened with the prairie chicken?"

"Sure enough is. I went out one mornin', and there it was, layin' right there on the step."

"How did the government agent explain that?"

"Said it was put there by somebody who felt guilty 'bout what he'd done. He was big on that idea, said it explained things just fine." Lindeman screwed his face up and said in a prissy voice, " 'A man who felt guilty would want to let people know about his crime. That way, he might achieve some measure of pardon.' "

I laughed. "But you don't believe that."

"Believe it, hell. I don't even know what it means."

I thought he might be joshing me just a little. He liked to play the small-town bumpkin, but he wasn't stupid by any means.

"What makes you so popular around here?" I asked him.

He frowned and hit the steering wheel with the palm of his hand. "That damn Linda."

"It wasn't anything that Linda said. Nobody in her place was interested in me at all until I sat down with you. Then they did everything they could to pretend that they weren't trying to figure out who I was."

"Yeah, it was pretty obvious, I guess. Lots of those fellas used to be good buddies of mine, but they won't hardly speak to me now. I guess you might've noticed that I was the only one in there who was sittin' by himself. Not countin' you, I mean. You'd think I had some kinda disease."

"Do you?"

His frown changed to a crooked grin. "Not that I know of. It's all because of that damn bird."

"Why don't you tell me about it, then?"

"Said I would, didn't I?"

I leaned back in the seat as if I were waiting and didn't say anything.

"Here's our turn," Lindeman said, pulling off the pavement onto a dirt road. "You know anything at all about birds? Any kind of birds?"

"Not much. I know they sing and build nests and eat worms."

He looked disgusted and waved a hand at the window. "What about coastal prairies?"

"Even less than about birds."

"You may be worse than that gover'ment fella after all."

I was afraid he might be right.

"When we get up to the house," he said, "I'm gonna try to get you educated."

I could hardly wait.

The house was a low-roofed ranch style sitting in a grove of tall shade trees, pecans and oaks. There weren't many other trees around, though I knew that not far away there were dense forests of natural growth.

Lindeman parked under one of the trees and got out. "Let's sit over there," he said, pointing to a couple of lawn chairs under a pecan tree.

We walked over and sat down. Lindeman pointed at the field of grass in front of us.

"What the gover'ment did here first was clear out some of the brush that'd grown up over the years, specially that Macartney rose."

"You can stop right there and start my education," I said.

"The Macartney rose is a bush that was brought over here and planted for some damn-fool reason or other, prob'ly because somebody thought it had pretty white flowers on it. And I guess the flowers *are* pretty if you like that sort of thing. Never did, myself. Or maybe the cattlemen wanted the rose thickets for windbreaks. Anyway, they grew like weeds and took over."

"Those things in the fields that we passed on the way here," I said. "They looked like big brush piles with white flowers all over them."

"That's Macartney rose, all right. Played hell with the bird habitat, is what it did, but nobody knew that for years. You let 'em go, they'll take over ever' acre you got."

"But there aren't any here on Lance's property."

"Like I said, they been cleared. That's part of what the gover'ment did. This place is pretty much like a natural prairie now, planted with mostly bluestem and gramma grass, stuff chickens like."

I looked out over the grass that bent just a little in the slight breeze. There were also wildflowers beginning to show their color, bluebonnets and Indian paintbrushes and others that I couldn't identify.

"And the prairie chickens are out there somewhere?"

"They're out there. We might get a look at some a 'em later. Plenty of other birds, too. The others are a lot easier to spot."

"You were going to show me the dead bird."

"In a minute. We're waitin' for somebody."

"Who?"

"There they come now," Lindeman said, pointing toward the dirt road.

I could see a big Ford coming in our direction. In less than a minute it pulled into the yard and parked beside Lindeman's Dodge. Anne got out on the passenger side.

She was wearing jeans and a red shirt, with her hair in a ponytail. I remembered that she'd been wearing jeans and a shirt like that the night of our high school graduation, and she'd put the robe on over them. But she'd been wearing her hair down. It had reached past her shoulders.

I flashed forward to the present and waited for the little guy in my chest to get out his sledgehammer and slug me in the heart. He didn't, and I decided that I had matured overnight.

Anne smiled at me, and I looked away from her at the driver of the car. He was short and compact and wearing a pair of wire-rimmed glasses. He was dressed differently from anyone I'd seen yet in Picketville: leather walking shoes, earth-tone canvas pants, a many-pocketed vest, and a wide-brimmed hat. A pair of black binoculars hung from a plastic strap around his neck. He looked as if he might have just stepped out of the Chickadee Nature Store.

"Lance says you know Anne," Lindeman said. "That little geek is Martin York. He's a bird-watcher."

That explained the getup. "I think they like to be called *birders*," I said. Might as well practice my political correctness.

"Don't see that it makes much difference," Lindeman said, not being a sensitive nineties guy like me.

I didn't see any need to correct him, because by that time Anne and York had reached us.

"Good morning, Tru, Dad," Anne said. "Tru, I'd like you to meet Martin York. He's going to help you with this. Martin, this is Truman Smith, an old friend."

I didn't recall having asked for any help, but York stuck out his hand, and I took it. He hadn't looked like the type to play macho games, so I wasn't prepared when he tried to crush my hand. I thought I caught a hint of a self-satisfied smile when I winced, but it vanished so quickly that I couldn't be sure.

"Glad to meet you, Smith," he said.

I retrieved my hand and didn't say a thing.

"We saw your buddies at the cafe while ago," Lindeman told York.

York turned from me and looked at him quizzically.

"Evans and his butt-boys. 'Scuse me, Anne."

Anne smiled at him. "I might have heard the term before."

"I hope it wasn't Paul that said it."

Anne laughed. "I don't remember."

"Forget the crude phraseology," York said. "What about Evans and his toadies?"

Obviously he was out to impress me with his vocabulary. Or maybe it was Anne he wanted to impress.

"They were in the cafe," Lindeman said. "They didn't say anything, just gave Smith a little bump and run. The usual intimidation stuff."

"Those bastards."

Then again, maybe he wasn't trying to impress anyone after all. He looked back at me. "Did he tell you they killed the bird?" he asked.

I shrugged. "Nobody ever tells me anything."

"It's kinda complicated," Lindeman said. "Why don't we go inside, and I'll see if I can tell it straight through."

That sounded like a good idea to me. I was getting tired of trying to figure out what was going on.

Lindeman led us into the house. The windows were open and it was dark and airy inside; Lindeman was as judicious in his use of air-conditioning as I was.

"It's kinda hard to know where to start," Lindeman said when we were inside and seated on chairs and a couch that were at least as old as the furniture in the Picketville Inn.

"Try starting at the beginning," I said. "That's usually the best place."

Lindeman shook his head. "Hard to say just exactly where that is."

"Start with Evans, then," I said.

I was getting interested in Evans. What kind of man needed bodyguards in a place like Picketville?

"I can tell you about Evans," Anne said. I must have looked surprised because she added, "I know him because of the radio station. Sometimes I think all this started at the radio station."

"Then that's the place to begin," I said.

Anne nodded. "It was Lance who wanted to put Evans on the air Paul was against it from the first."

"As well he should have been," York said. He'd taken off his hat and binoculars, and I'd learned that he was bald except for a fringe of hair around the sides of his head. "Evans is a lunatic."

"I oon't think so," I said. "I heard him last night. He's shrewd, he knows his audience, and he's done his home-work. He may have some pretty weird ideas, but he's not a lunatic."

York's mouth twisted sourly. "Are you one of those gun nuts?"

"I own a gun."

"I might have known."

"I don't have it on me, though," I said.

"Boys, boys," Anne said. "We're getting off the subject."

She was right, and I was a little nettled that I'd let York get under my skin so easily. I'd taken an instant dislike to him, and I didn't know why. Unless it was the fact that he'd been in the car alone with Anne. Could it be that I was jealous? Maybe the maturity I'd achieved overnight was already slipping away.

"Paul fought against putting Evans on the air," Anne said, trying to get back on the subject. "He didn't like what Evans had to say, and he didn't think there was any audience for a show like Evans wanted to do."

"But there was," I said.

"There certainly was, and Lance was sure of it all along. He doesn't agree with Evans's philosophy, but he does believe in freedom of speech. And, of course, he believes in making money. KLWG has a pretty powerful transmitter for such a small town, and it doesn't cut its power at night. People can pick up Evans's show all over the area, and that includes most of Houston. They love Ralph Evans in Houston. Lance gets a lot of advertising money from there."

"If everybody loves Evans, why does he need bodyguards?" I asked.

"Evans has had death threats." Anne looked at York. "Or so he tells everyone. Of course, there's always the possibility that he's just saying that to create an image."

"*I* certainly never threatened him," York said.

It was true that he didn't look like the type to threaten anyone, but then he didn't look like the type who'd try to crush your hand when he shook it, either.

"That ain't exactly the truth," Lindeman said. "You told me you were goin' to kill the son of a bitch. 'Scuse me, Anne."

"I just said that in the heat of the moment," York said. "After I found out about the dead bird. I didn't mean anything by it, and besides, Evans had his bodyguards a long time before that."

York looked even less likely to kill someone than he did to make threats. But sometimes the unlikeliest suspects were the ones you had to pay the most attention to.

But we were rambling again, so I said, "We're getting way off the track here. If nobody's going to tell this story straight, maybe I could just get some answers to a few questions."

Everyone looked at me, and Lindeman said, "You go ahead, then."

Great. I had their attention, and now all I had to do was figure out which questions to ask. It's never easy.

9

I DECIDED TO begin with something I'd been wondering about.

"Where did Lance find Ralph Evans?" I asked Anne. "He doesn't sound like a trained broadcaster."

"He's not," Anne said. "He was doing a show on some little twenty-five-hundred-watt station in East Texas. Lance heard him while he was on a fishing trip and thought Evans was a diamond in the rough."

"So he brought him here to us," York said. "To fill the air waves with culture and enlightenment. And we all lived happily ever after."

I was beginning to like York less and less. "You think he killed the prairie chicken. Why?"

York looked at Lindeman and then at Anne, rolling his eyes as if I were an escapee from a home for the mentally disadvantaged.

"Isn't it obvious?" he asked.

"Not to me," I said.

"You said that you listened to him last night. Did

you hear his commercial for Spotted Owl in a Can?"

I said that I had.

York shrugged. "There you have it, then."

"Have what? The commercial was just a joke."

"If you think that, you haven't heard his spiel on the new laws regarding the government's right to protect endangered species by requiring landowners to do certain things with their property. Or to refrain from doing certain things."

"No, I haven't heard that."

"Well, of course he's opposed to the government's being able to do *anything* to protect any species. He believes a landowner should be able to do whatever he wants with his property. If he wants to kill all the dodos on it, he should just do it. And Evans has had a few things to say about Lance's good work with the prairie chickens, believe me. It's a wonder the town hasn't marched out here with torches and burned the fields."

"He's attacked his employer?" I asked.

"He attacks everyone he doesn't agree with," Anne said. "Verbally, of course. Lance doesn't mind; that's what Evans's show is all about. Freedom of speech, remember?"

"Freedom of speech doesn't have anything to do with killing birds," I said.

"No, and Evans knows that speech can go only so far," York said. "He saw that talking about Garrison's ranch wasn't going to do any good, so he decided on more direct action and killed that bird. Or he had one of his bodyguards do it. Or some of the others in their group. Either way, he's behind it."

"Do you have any evidence of that?"

York just looked smug and stubborn. "I know what I know."

There's nothing harder to penetrate than a closed mind, so I gave up on York and turned to Lindeman. "You agree with York?"

"Yeah, I guess I do. I think Evans was makin' a statement

or something. He got plenty of publicity out of it, too. There was a big article about the bird in the paper, and it mentioned Evans's radio show. People wrote letters to the editor for a week."

"What kind of letters?"

"Mostly about how it was a dumb idea to put birds ahead of people. Ever'body around here figures the gover'ment should be doin' something for the rice farmers instead of some bird."

"Did anybody come out on the bird's side?"

"You saw how people acted this mornin' at the cafe," Lindeman said. "They know what I think, and they don't like it. They don't want to mess with Evans or his gang, and they don't want to have anything to do with somebody who does. Besides, they like what he has to say, and the fact is, nobody cares much about prairie chickens."

"I care," York told him. "Anne cares, and so do Laurel and Bob."

"Laurel and Bob?" I said.

"The Greers," Anne said. "They're birders, like Martin."

If they were like Martin, I wasn't sure I'd care to meet them.

"What's this about a gang?" I asked. "And a group? Is there someone I should know about besides Evans and the two bodyguards?"

Lindeman said, "There's a bunch around here, calls itself the Picketville Minute Men. It's a sort of militia group, but it's not all that well organized. Evans heads it up, along with Gar and Bert. They like to go off on the weekends and do survival stuff out in the country, shoot their guns and all that kind of thing. They march in the Fourth of July parade."

"Do they hunt, or just shoot?"

"They aren't hunters," York said. "Killers is what they are."

"They never killed anybody as far as I know," Lindeman said.

York said, "They killed that bird."

York had a one-track mind. It was time to get on another track, if I could.

"How are things at the radio station?" I asked Anne. "What does your husband think about the dead prairie chicken?"

"Things are pretty tense. Paul and Evans didn't get along well from the first, and now they don't get along at all. Evans knows that Paul tried to keep him off the station, and he's always been resentful. After the prairie chicken was killed, Paul tried to get Lance to pull the show. He and Evans had quite a confrontation about it at the station."

"Define 'confrontation,' " I said.

"There was a loud argument and some pushing and shoving."

"Where were the bodyguards?"

"They got into it, too. Paul got away from them just before things got completely out of hand and locked himself in his office."

It sounded as if Evans and his associates were a little on the unruly side.

"But Evans is still working at the station," I said.

Anne nodded. "Lance doesn't want him off. He's bringing in too much advertising."

Good old Lance. "But it's his bird that's dead. He must not think Evans killed it, or he wouldn't have hired me."

"Hard to say what he thinks," Lindeman said. "He told me that if you could prove Evans did it, he'd pull the show. But not unless you had rock-solid proof. Could be he's scared of Evans, too."

I wondered if Anne had noticed the implications of the "too," but when I looked at her, she gave no indication.

"About this dead bird," I said. "I guess it's time to have a look at it."

"I've already seen it, thank you," York said.

"So has Anne," Lindeman told me. "You come on with me out to the back room and we'll look in the deep freeze."

I got up and followed him to a small room behind the kitchen. The room held a large built-in cupboard and an upright freezer.

Lindeman opened the freezer and a thin white fog rolled out into the room and drifted toward the floor. Lindeman reached inside the freezer and brought out something in a large plastic bag.

"You ever hear the joke about the parrot in the deep freeze?" he asked me.

"No. Do I want to?"

"Maybe not, but ever' time I get out this bird, I think about it. Guy named Womack told it to me. Seems there was this woman who buys a parrot to keep her company, but when she gets it home she finds out that all it does is cuss. So she calls the pet store and threatens to bring it back, but the owner says there's a way to take care of the cussin'. Tells her to put the parrot in the deep freeze for five minutes, not long enough to kill him or anything, but just to give him a shock. Tells her that'll cure the cussin'. Well, she tries it, just takes him and pops him in. And when she opens the deep freeze five minutes later, the parrot has frost all over him. He's shaking and his wings are wrapped all around him, and his beak is chatterin'. 'Why'd you do that to me?' he asks her, so she tells him. He points with his wing over to a corner of the freezer and says, 'If you did that to me for cussin' then what did that goddamn chicken do?'"

I laughed. It wasn't all that funny, but how often do you hear a parrot joke?

"Let's go in the kitchen," Lindeman said. "Light's better in there."

We went into the other room, where he opened the bag

and brought out the frozen bird. He put it on the kitchen table and said, "What do you think?"

"I think it doesn't look much like a chicken," I said, and it didn't. It was sort of a dull brown with darker bars. It had a small crest of feathers and longer feathers that seemed to fall down its neck.

"It's not a chicken," Lindeman said. "It's—"

"—a grouse. Yeah. I know that."

There were dark flecks of blood on the bird and I could see where some of the feathers had been torn away.

"Twelve-gauge shotgun," Lindeman said. He picked up the plastic bag and shook it. Something rattled in the bottom. "I picked the shot out."

The shot wouldn't do us any good. It wasn't like a bullet. There was no way to identify the gun it had been fired from.

I poked the bird with my finger. It was stiff and hard. "And you and York think that Evans killed it."

"Him or his pals, Thornton and Ware. Yeah. They did it. Just their way of lettin' us know what they think of savin' an endangered species."

It was possible, I supposed, but I still didn't see the point of it. Evans might not like the idea of a government-protected bird, but Lance was still the man with the money and the radio station. It didn't make sense to me that Evans would want to make an enemy of someone in Lance's position.

"Has anyone talked to Evans about the bird?" I asked.

"I did," Lindeman said. "So did Lance. Evans said he didn't have a thing to do with it."

"But you didn't believe him."

"You wouldn't either if you talked to him. Smiled that little smile of his, and those two apes stood right by him and grinned like shit-eatin' dogs."

"I guess I'll have to have my own little talk with him," I

said. I didn't relish the idea. I didn't know about Bert Ware, but I was sure Gar Thornton was bad news. Just thinking about him reminded me of the stingray.

"Good luck to you," Lindeman said. "And watch out for Gar and Bert. They don't like anybody to get too close to him."

"I'll bet."

Gar could keep people away, all right. He could probably crush my head like a cardboard box.

Lindeman put the bird back in the bag and returned it to the freezer. Then we went back to where Anne and York were sitting.

"Aren't you going to show Tru the birds?" Anne asked when we came into the room. "He needs to see them to get an idea of what the ranch is like and why it's so important."

"I'll take him right now," Lindeman said. "Do you two want to come along?"

York did, but Anne said that she had to get back to town. Since she was riding with York, he would have to drive her. He was disappointed at missing the opportunity to show off his knowledge of birds, but he managed to keep a stiff upper lip. No wonder. He'd be alone in the car with Anne. I would have traded places with him in a nanosecond if it had been possible.

Before they left, Anne said, "Why don't you show him the barns first, Red, and tell him a little about the prairie chicken's feeding and mating habits. You never know what might prove useful."

Lindeman said he would. York put on his hat, picked up his binoculars, and hung them around his neck.

"All right," he said. "I'm ready."

Lindeman and I followed him and Anne outside and watched them drive away.

"That York's not all bad," Lindeman said. "He's just a little snooty."

I thought about York being in the car alone with Anne. I wondered if she thought he was snooty.

"I guess that's one word for it," I said.

"You got a better one?"

"Not right on the tip of my tongue," I told him. "Let's go see those barns."

THE BARNS WERE just barns, made mostly of metal, with high, airy roofs. One held a couple of Italian-made tractors and a truck even older and more battered than Lindeman's Dodge. Lindeman explained that the tractors were used for mowing and plowing.

"We plant a little maize," he said. "But we buy most of what we feed. The chickens like grasshoppers, too, and there are plenty of those."

"What's in the other barn?"

"Grain. That's about it, that and the rats the cats don't catch."

"You keep cats?"

"They don't get out after the birds, if that's what's botherin' you. Let's go have a look."

The cats were lying in the shade under an overhanging roof. One was a calico female, and the other was gray, a neutered tom. They lay without moving, watching us through slitted eyes.

"Elvis and Priscilla," Lindeman said.

"I thought they split up a long time ago."

"Not these two. Best little ratters around. Keep this place as clean as a whistle."

He unlocked the door to the storeroom and we went inside. The cats watched but didn't follow. Lindeman switched on a light, and dust motes drifted through its beams and filled my nose. I resisted the urge to sneeze as I looked around at the neatly stacked sacks of grain. As far as I could tell, there weren't any rats.

"See what I mean?" Lindeman said.

I saw that the barn was clean and rat-free. But I was more interested in seeing a prairie chicken. I said, "What about that tour of the ranch?"

Lindeman switched off the lights. "Comin' right up," he said.

10

THE RANCH ROAD was nothing but hard-packed ruts, and we bounced along in the Dodge with Lindeman pointing out the sights, not that there was much to see. Mostly there was just prairie, and grass, and wildflowers, though I glimpsed some trees off in the distance.

"We'll be comin' up on the marsh in a minute or so," Lindeman said. "I'll stop a good way off so we can get out and have a look. Don't want to scare off any of the birds."

"I didn't know that prairie chickens were waterbirds," I said.

"They aren't. We're not goin' to see any prairie chickens yet, they're shy and as hard as hell to find. But there's all kinds of birds out here. Give old Ralph a chance, and he'd shotgun ever' last one of 'em."

We drove very slowly up a slight rise, and I could see the trunk and branches of a rotten tree sticking up. There was a bird of some kind on one of the bare limbs.

"That's an anhinga crane," Lindeman said when I touched his arm.

We topped the rise, and the broad marsh was spread out in front of us. I was taken completely by surprise at what I saw. Hundreds of birds skittered along its edges or waded in its shallow water. It was almost like a scene from an old Tarzan movie, one of the Technicolor ones.

"Kinda gets you, don't it?" Lindeman said. "People don't ever expect to see something like that right out here in the middle of what looks like a wasteland."

"How many different kinds of birds are out there?" I asked.

I couldn't identify a single one of them. York would have held me in utter contempt.

"Let's get out and have a look," Lindeman said, stopping the truck.

We got out, closing the doors as softly as we could, and just stood there for a second. The sun was warm on my face, and I could hear grasshoppers jumping in the dry grass nearby and the faint buzz of an airplane so far away that it was just a dark speck against the single white cloud in the bright blue sky. The birds made no noise at all.

"All right, now," Lindeman said. "Look through your binoculars and focus on those pink birds way over by the far side."

Before we'd left the ranch house, Lindeman had gone back inside and brought out two pairs of 7X35 binoculars, one for me and one for him. They weren't the most expensive you could buy, but they would do. I put the binoculars to my eyes and followed orders.

"Those are spoonbills," Lindeman said. "I bet you recognize 'em now."

I didn't recognize them, not really, but I saw the spoon-shaped bills that gave them their name.

"There's some blue herons out there," Lindeman said. "And some snowy egrets and cormorants. Those things scootin' around on the mud are called stilts. Of course, there's a couple of kinds of ducks, too, and there's some white ibis. Let's walk on down the road and see what else I can pick out for you."

I didn't bother to tell him that he'd been going much too fast for me. He probably knew it already. I let the binoculars dangle from the strap and followed him down the right-hand rut.

"You don't look much like an expert on birds," I said.

"You mean I don't look like Martin York? Hell, you don't have to wear a getup like his to look at birds. 'Course that vest is pretty nice when you're gonna be out in the field for a while. You can carry you a granola bar or a package of cheese crackers in those pockets, along with your knife and your snake-bite kit."

"Snake-bite kit? There are snakes around here?"

"Yep. Cottonmouths, mostly. And alligators, too."

Suddenly I wanted to get back in the truck. Alligators I can deal with. They're big enough for me to see if they're anywhere around. But snakes are a different story. I really don't like snakes.

"Don't worry," Lindeman said. Maybe he could see that I'd broken out in a mild sweat. "The snakes stick pretty close to the water. We won't be gettin' that close to it."

"That's fine with me," I said, feeling a little better about things. But not much.

As we walked along the road, which was built up like a dam that ran around the edge of the marsh in a semicircle, I could hear the sound of the airplane getting closer. I looked up, shading my eyes with my hand.

"Looks like Billy Younger's little crop duster," Lindeman said. "The white crop dusters are all owned by private individuals. The yellow ones are corporate-owned."

I watched as the little white plane flew closer, wondering what it was doing up there. I wasn't the only one.

"I wonder what he's doing up there?" Lindeman said.

"Not supposed to be flyin' around here. That's one of the things about this place the gover'ment made sure of before Lance worked his deal with 'em. There's not supposed to be any dustin' within twenty miles of here, and even that's too damn close. If there was to be any over spray, it'd wipe out ever' bird here. Polecats and possums, too."

"Maybe he's just up for a ride. It's a nice day."

"Billy don't go up for rides. That aviation gas costs too much for that kinda stuff. He's gonna scare the birds if he don't veer off."

He didn't exactly veer off. Instead, he made a long, looping turn, then pointed the nose of the plane in the same direction we were headed. If he kept coming, he would soon be directly over our heads.

I looked back down, not because I heard anything but more because of something I seemed to feel, like a sudden vibration in the ground. And I saw something that I didn't quite understand. The rut behind Lindeman's Dodge was exploding upward as clods of dirt jumped into the air and the ground ripped itself apart.

I threw myself into Lindeman, dragging him off his feet and pulling him toward me as I rolled down the side of the road. The ground crushed the binoculars against my chest.

The plane buzzed past above us, and bits of dirt stung my face as the rut erupted where we had been standing. After a couple of turns we flopped into the mud below the road, and Lindeman shoved himself away from me.

"What the hell are you doin'?" he said. "Have you gone nuts?"

"Somebody's shooting at us," I said. "From the plane."

He looked at me. "Huh?"

"Shooting at us." I looked up at the plane, which had made another turn and was coming back in our direction. "Here he comes again."

I still couldn't hear the gun, but water and mud were splashing up from the marsh. Birds were flapping wildly, some of them taking to the air. One spoonbill collapsed into the water, feathers and blood flying as a bullet pierced its body.

"Goddamn!" Lindeman yelled, and we buried our faces in the mud, as if that would help. Maybe it did. Neither of us was hit, although lead thunked into the mud beside us, spattering it all over us.

Just before I turned away, I got a look at what was shooting at us. Some kind of semiautomatic weapon with a suppressor on the muzzle hung over the edge of the cockpit. I couldn't see who was holding it, however.

"He's gonna kill us," Lindeman said, pulling his face up to take a breath. "If the birds don't get him first."

There were hardly any birds left on the water now, and they were soaring higher and higher. The pilot must have realized the danger, but he wasn't discouraged. He made another turn and started back.

"We have to get into the water," I said. "We might have a chance there, if it's deep enough."

I stood up, dragging Lindeman to his feet, and we jogged across the flat with the mud slapping and sucking under our feet. The binoculars bounced wildly, slamming into my breastbone.

Or maybe what I felt was my heart, slamming into my breastbone from the other side. I wasn't able to make any fine distinctions at the moment.

It must have been the binoculars, however, because Lindeman tore his off, pulling the strap over his head and sending his Astros cap flying into the air. He threw the binoculars aside and kept running.

The cap landed in front of me. I stepped on it and crushed it into the slick mud as I tossed my own binoculars away, and we splashed through the shallows, trying to get to water deep enough to cover us.

The plane swooped by and bullets splatted into the water around us, sending little geysers into the air. I launched myself forward in a flat dive as something tugged at my sweatshirt, and I heard Lindeman scream just before I went under.

The water I landed in wasn't much more than eighteen inches deep, no protection at all, really, but at least I was covered, and that gave me the illusion of invisibility. I stayed down as long as I could hold my breath and then came up to look for Lindeman.

I didn't see him, but I did see a red stain spreading on top of the muddy water a few yards away. I spit out a mouthful of water and mud and looked for the plane. It was heading off to the north and was already so far away that it looked no larger than a model plane hanging from a kid's ceiling. The birds were too high and too thick in the air for it to risk making another pass at us.

I sloshed over to the red stain and reached down into the water. I felt Lindeman's shirt, grabbed a handful of cloth, and pulled him to the surface. He was unconscious, but I didn't think he was dead. Blood was flowing down his leg along with the muddy water.

I hadn't seen a hospital in Picketville, and I didn't even know if there were any doctors there. There probably wasn't time to drive Lindeman to town, anyway. I had to do something for him now.

I pulled him free of the water and over to the side of the road. Both of us were soaking wet and covered with mud, and my hands were shaking. I didn't like being shot at, and I was afraid the plane might come back as soon as the birds cleared out.

The birds didn't leave, however. They weren't nearly as disturbed by what had happened as I was. They were already settling back down on the lake, but if the plane came back they would fly up much more quickly than they had before. I hoped. And I hoped the pilot was thinking the same way that I was.

I didn't carry a knife, so I couldn't cut Lindeman's pants off. I had to take them off. That wasn't easy. They fit him loosely, but they were wet and clingy, and Lindeman wasn't any help.

It was a struggle, but I finally got them down around his knees. That was far enough. I could see that he'd been shot through the fleshy part of his right thigh, and the bullet had gone right through. Blood was still seeping out, but that was a good sign, I thought. No major arteries had been severed.

It might still be a good idea to try to stop the bleeding, so I slid Lindeman's belt off and tied it above the wound, then pulled his pants back up. There wasn't much else I could do except get him to the truck and back to the ranch. The wound had to be cleaned and disinfected.

Lindeman wasn't a small man, and it was quite a struggle to get him to the truck. I didn't think we'd walked far from the old Dodge, but as I hauled Lindeman along the ruts, gripping him under the armpits and pulling him along with his heels dragging, I realized we had walked at least ten miles.

Or maybe it just seemed that way. I had to stop once and rest, but when we finally got to the truck, I managed to bundle Lindeman into the passenger seat.

I looked in the ignition for the keys, and they were there. Lindeman hadn't been worried about car thieves. At least that was one thing to be thankful for.

I got him as close to upright as I could and kept him there by fastening his seat and shoulder belt around him. He didn't look good, but he was still breathing.

I started the truck and headed back to the house.

11

LINDEMAN CAME TO as the truck bounced along the ruts. The first thing he did was wince in pain.

"Jesus H. Mahogany Christ!" he said. He started to grab his leg, but resisted. He took a deep breath through gritted teeth and leaned back against the seat, his eyes tightly closed.

He let out the breath slowly, and after awhile he asked, "What the hell happened?"

I gave him the short answer. "You got shot."

He seemed almost relieved. "You sure that's all it is?"

"I'm sure. What else could it be?"

"I hurt so damn much, I was afraid I'd been snake-bit. Those cottonmouths can kill you quicker'n a bullet."

I'd forgotten about the snakes. Getting shot at from a plane has a tendency to drive other considerations out of my head.

"How bad is it?" Lindeman asked, looking down at his leg.

"I'm no doctor, but I think it's a minor wound."

"Is that like minor surgery?"

"That's right. Because you have it, it's minor. If I'd been shot in the same place, it would be a major wound."

He tried a grin that he couldn't quite bring off, sucked in a breath, and said, "That's what I figured."

If he could joke about it, he must have been feeling a lot better than I would have under the same circumstances.

"The bullet went straight through your leg. I've got your belt tied around it."

"We better loosen it now and then."

"We can do that as soon as we get back to the house. Do you have any hydrogen peroxide around?"

"There's some in the medicine cabinet. We can pour some on me, but I think we oughta go to a doctor unless you're a lot better at this stuff than I am."

"I'm not."

"What I figured. What the hell was that all about, do you think?"

"I don't have any idea," I said.

"THEY WERE TRYIN' to kill us," Lindeman said later.

He was sitting in his living room with a bottle of Coors in his right hand. He had his leg propped up on the coffee table. I wasn't sure he should be having the beer, but he was. I had a glass of water. Lindeman didn't have any Big Red on hand.

We were both less muddy than we'd been earlier. There was a laundry room in the back of the house, so I was able to wash and dry my jeans and sweatshirt. I'd taken a shower, too, after I'd cleaned Lindeman's wound and bandaged his leg with some tape, pads, and gauze he had in his bathroom. He was able to get in the shower, and I'd gotten most of the mud off of him. Before the shower, he'd taken a handful of ibuprofen tablets, which is why I was worried about the beer.

And he'd changed his mind about the doctor.

"That'll mean we have to bring the sheriff in on this," he said. "The doctor'll have to report the bullet wound, and I don't have anything to say to that son of a bitch Sheriff Roy Peavy."

"Why not?"

"Because he's in Evans's hip pocket. They're practically best friends. Peavy likes the Minute Men. Thinks they keep down crime around here."

"Well, it's too late to keep him out of it. I called the sheriff's department while you were cleaning up. Peavy's going to meet us at the doctor's office."

That wasn't the only call I'd made. I'd tried to get hold of Lance, but I couldn't get past his secretary. She didn't care who I was or why I wanted him. He was in "an important meeting," and he'd given orders not to be disturbed. She didn't care if the Chinese army had invaded Picketville and killed everyone in town; she wasn't going to disturb Lance Garrison.

Lindeman wasn't happy with me. "Maybe we can tell Peavy it was some kind of accident. Deal with Evans ourselves."

"Maybe Evans wasn't the one shooting at us. I couldn't see who was in the plane. Could you?"

"Hell, no. But it was Evans. Who the hell else is goin' to be up in an airplane with an automatic rifle?"

I didn't have an answer for that. In fact, there were quite a few things I didn't have answers for. There was a lot more going on here than a dead prairie chicken, though, I knew that much.

"Did you call the doctor, too?"

"Dr. Harvey. You said he was the one you used."

"I don't use him all that much. I don't hardly ever get sick."

"You're not sick now, either. You're shot." I looked at my watch. "We'd better go."

Lindeman put his leg on the floor and tried to get off the couch without help. He couldn't quite do it.

"Hoo-eee," he said, sitting back down before I could get to him. "There's a walking stick in the hall closet, used to belong to my grandpa. I'd appreciate it if you'd get it for me."

I looked in the closet and found the cane stuck in the back. I took it to Lindeman and helped him stand up. He balanced himself with the aid of the cane and took two shaky steps forward, wincing each time his foot touched the floor.

"I guess I can make it to the truck," he said. "You better stand close by, though."

I walked beside him, holding his arm, and we got to the truck without incident. I helped Lindeman in, and he said, "You're really gonna like Sheriff Peavy."

"I'll bet," I said.

DR. HARVEY SAW Lindeman as soon as we arrived at his office. I sat in the waiting room and read a tattered five-year-old issue of *U. S. News & World Report* and waited for the sheriff while the receptionist watched me suspiciously. She probably thought I was going to steal the magazine, which would have been a shame. It was the only magazine in the office. The only other thing for the patients to read was a coverless paperback historical novel called *Rivers of Gold*.

Peavy came in with his deputy. They were both tall, and they both wore ten-gallon white hats. The difference was that the deputy wore his with a uniform, while Peavy wore a Western-cut suit and a bolo tie.

I could see the bulge of a pistol under the side of Peavy's jacket, but the deputy was covered with peace-keeping equipment. There was a radio on his shoulder, and besides a pistol, his belt held Mace and a thick black baton. "Be Prepared," that's the Boy Scout motto.

Peavy said hello to the receptionist, who smiled and asked how he was. She obviously looked on him much more kindly than she did me. Then Peavy turned to me and asked if I was Smith.

"That's right."

The deputy looked at me with red-rimmed eyes. I wondered if he'd been up all night chasing criminals.

"I'm Ward Peavy," the sheriff said. "And this is Deputy Denbow. You'd better come with us."

It wasn't that I didn't want to tell Peavy what had happened. It was just that I didn't feel like going anywhere.

"Why can't we talk here?" I asked.

"I'd like to talk to you somewhere a little less public," Peavy said.

"I have to take Mr. Lindeman home after the doctor examines him."

"Don't you worry about that. I'll see that Deputy Denbow here does that little job for you."

Deputy Denbow smiled and showed me a set of teeth that demonstrated a marked lack of orthodontic care.

"I'll take real good care of the old man," he said.

For some reason I didn't believe him. Maybe it was the eyes. Maybe the smile.

"I'd rather stay here until I'm sure he's all right," I said. "I told him I'd wait."

Peavy shrugged. "If that's the way you feel about it. We can sit down here and talk if that's all right with Jean."

He smiled at the receptionist, who said it was fine with her. There wasn't anyone else there to overhear us. We sat in the straight, uncomfortable chairs, and I told Peavy and his deputy exactly what had happened.

"And it was Red that said the plane belonged to Billy Younger?" the deputy asked.

I don't know whether he was trying to trick me or whether he was just stupid. If I'd been a betting man, I'd have gone with stupid, though.

"I've never been in this town before in my life," I said. "How would I know whose plane it was?"

"No need to get touchy with Deputy Denbow," Peavy said. "He doesn't know much about you. But we're having you checked out."

I'd figured they might.

"We heard about you already, though," Denbow said.

So he wasn't stupid. He was just suspicious.

"About that business you got mixed up in not far from here," Peavy explained. "With the alligator."

I wasn't surprised that they'd heard about that. The bad news was that I'd had some trouble with the law-enforcement people on that job. And the law-enforcement people had had some trouble with me.

"We know the kind of fella you are," Denbow said. He was sitting on my right, and he smelled like an ashtray that someone had forgotten to empty. "You're a wiseass. And you like to cause trouble."

"Look," I said, trying to sound earnest and reasonable and anything but a wiseass, "I don't want to cause any trouble, and I don't want to be a wiseass. I just came out here to see about a dead bird. That's all. I've never been here before, and I don't know Billy Younger or what his plane looks like."

"Maybe not," Peavy said.

"Why don't you ask him?"

Peavy shook his head. "Well, you see, that's the hard part. Billy can't talk right now."

"Why not?"

"Because somebody hit him in the head and tied him up in his hangar," Denbow said. "Hit him pretty damn hard, too. He's on his way to the hospital in Houston."

Peavy and Denbow were no slouches. I'd told them about Younger on the phone, and they'd already had somebody check on him.

"His plane's gone, though," Denbow said. "So you may be right about that part."

"Any sign of who did it?" I asked.

"Billy couldn't tell us much," Peavy said. "He remembers two men getting out of a truck with stocking masks that mashed their faces all out of shape. They were wearing camouflage outfits, but then a lot of folks go rigged out like that around here."

That was probably true, but I immediately connected the camo suits with Ralph Evans and his bodyguards. I didn't mention that to Peavy, however. He could figure it out for himself if he cared to.

"Did Younger tell you anything else?" I asked.

Peavy said, "The two men held guns on him and made him get out his plane. Then one of them hit him in the head. That's about all he remembers, but we'll talk to him again when he's feeling better. We'll keep after it until we find out who's responsible."

Denbow was looking at me as if I were someone whose "Wanted" poster he'd seen come across his desk.

"I didn't steal the plane," I told him. "I didn't shoot at myself, either."

Denbow turned to Peavy and said, "See what I mean about him bein' a wiseass?"

"I don't mean to be," I said. "But the two of you are questioning me as if I had something to do with what happened. I'm as much in the dark as you are."

"Maybe so, but we can't be sure of that, can we?" Peavy said.

"You can take my word for it."

Denbow laughed, but at least he didn't call me a wiseass again.

"One thing we know for sure," Peavy said. "We know you came here to make trouble about that dead bird. The government's already decided that that was just an accident. We don't need you here trying to stir things up."

"I'm not stirring things up. I didn't get here until last night. I haven't even talked to anyone in town."

"Well, somebody knows you're here," Denbow said. "And they don't like you worth a damn."

I could tell by the look on his face that he didn't like me worth a damn, either, but I didn't see any profit in calling his attention to the fact.

Peavy was about to add something to the discussion, but Lindeman came out of the examining room just then. He was in a wheelchair pushed by a gray-haired nurse.

"Dr. Harvey says I got to get me some crutches," Lindeman said. "How are you doin', Peavy? Deputy Denbow?"

They said they were fine, and Peavy asked him to give his version of the events. Lindeman told it almost exactly as I had. While he was talking, an old man with a bad cough came in and was shown to the examining room. Dr. Harvey's practice wasn't going to make him rich.

"I guess that's it," Lindeman said when he was finished. "Anybody ask Billy Younger about the plane?"

Peavy said, "It was his, all right." He went on to fill him in.

"You know who it was, even if Billy can't tell you yet," Lindeman said. "Don't you?"

"Are you about to make an accusation?" Peavy asked. "You'd better be careful what you say."

"Then I don't have anything to say. You wouldn't believe me, anyhow."

Denbow licked his lips. "What do you mean by that?"

"Nothin'," Lindeman said. "I think I better go on home. My leg's hurtin' me pretty bad."

I stood up and got behind the wheelchair. "Where can we get some crutches?" I asked.

"There's a little medical-supply place not far from here," Lindeman said. "Push me out of here."

"What about it, Sheriff?" I said.

"All right. We don't have anything else to ask you right now. You can leave."

I pushed the wheelchair over to the door and we went out. I could feel Denbow's eyes on me all the way.

12

I TOOK LINDEMAN to the medical-supply store and we
picked up the crutches. He was awkward on them at first, but
managed to get out of the store and to the truck without falling
down. I helped him in and got him seated, then got behind
the wheel.

When I started the truck, Lindeman said, "Peavy won't
look for that airplane."

"Why not?"

"'Cause he knows it was Evans who stole it. There's
bound to be at least one of those Minute Men who can fly it,
and if Evans asked 'em to drop the A-bomb on downtown
Houston, they'd do it."

"Where do you think the plane would be if they were the
ones who took it?"

"I'll have to give that some thought. You plannin' to look
for it?"

I didn't know the answer to that one, not yet. I was still
trying to make all the things that had happened fit together
somehow, and I wasn't having much success.

Then Lindeman said he was hungry. I hadn't had anything to eat since breakfast, and neither had he.

"The Toole Shed?" I asked.

"Just about the only place in town, unless you want to eat at the Dairy Queen."

"The Toole Shed is fine. Are you sure you feel up to it?"

"Yeah. Dr. Harvey gave me some pills. He said they'd make me sleepy, but I didn't take one yet. That ibuprofen's doin' the job. I'm not hurtin' much."

Well, it was his leg. He could be brave about it if he wanted to.

My Chevy was still in the parking lot at The Toole Shed. I pulled up near the front door of the cafe and let Red get out of the Dodge, then parked by the Chevy. Red was balanced inexpertly on the crutches when I walked back to him, his foot just a little off the ground.

"I don't like these damn things even a little bit," he said. "I couldn't run if I wanted to."

I held the door of The Toole Shed open for him, and the odor of fried food rolled over me.

"Maybe you won't have to run again for a while," I said.

"Will if that damn Evans gets after me."

He clumped over to the nearest table and sat down with my help, leaning his crutches on the chair to his right. There were only a few other customers, and they all averted their eyes after one curious glance in our direction. While we were looking at the menus, Linda came over to take our order.

"What happened to you?" she asked Lindeman.

He looked up from his menu. "You wouldn't believe me if I told you."

She held her pencil poised over her order pad. "Try me."

"Guy shot me from an airplane," Lindeman said.

"You're right. I don't believe you. Now, what'll you have to eat?"

The menu was a little light on heart-healthy items, so I ordered a chicken-fried steak with Texas toast, mashed potatoes, and cream gravy. Lindeman decided on the meat loaf.

While we waited for the food to arrive, I asked Lindeman if he'd thought any more about why anyone would be shooting at us.

"Like I told you, I think they were tryin' to kill us," he said. "Except I don't think they were after *us*. I think they were after *you*."

"Me? Why me?"

"You're the one Lance brought in to see who killed his prairie chicken. You're the one Evans wants to get rid of."

I wasn't sure that Evans knew who I was, but this was a small town. I'd been checked into the motel by a guy who had been told by his boss who I was and maybe what I was doing there. The guy had one of Evans's bumper stickers on his car and had been listening to Evans's radio show. So it was certainly possible that Evans knew all about me.

I said to Lindeman, "You really seem convinced that it's Evans."

"Who else? If you find out it was him that killed that endangered bird, he's gonna be in deep shit with the feds and Lance is goin' to pull his show right off the air. Guys like Evans don't mind bein' in trouble. They're used to it. But they don't want to lose their show."

"And you think he'd kill to keep it."

"Damn right. Don't you?"

"I don't know Evans. And murder is a lot worse than killing a bird."

"You don't know much about how guys like Evans think, do you?"

I guessed I didn't, and I said so.

"The thing is," Lindeman said, "that they don't think like

you and me. They think they got a right to do just about any damn thing they please and that the Constitution guarantees 'em that right. They think the gover'ment's out to get rid of the Constitution, take all their freedoms away. They're downright paranoid about it."

There was no question that what I'd heard of Evans's show had a strong thread of paranoia running through it. The concentration camp idea hadn't been the only thing.

Lindeman toyed with the saltshaker. "The people who listen to Evans don't like lettin' anybody know anything about their lives. You know how they ask you to give your Social Security number when you renew your driver's license? The people who listen to Evans don't do it. I've heard 'em say they'll just stop drivin' first. Or drive without a license. They don't want to be in any more computer data bases."

They might have a point there. I was making a living on the fact that it was awfully easy to use a computer to find out things about people.

Lindeman went on. "The ones around here that go along with Evans's ideas haven't moved off to the mountains to live by themselves in a little one-room cabin, not yet, but they encourage other people to do it. And they think they have a right to do whatever they have to in defense of their freedoms. Even if it means killin' you and me. Which is what they tried to do today. Case closed."

I was beginning to think that Dino was right, not that I'd ever doubted him. Lance Garrison was still an asshole. It seemed that he'd gotten me into something that was much worse than he'd made it appear.

It was even possible that he was trying to use me to get rid of Evans for him. He might believe in freedom of speech, as Anne said, but that didn't mean that he might not be uncomfortable with the idea of having Evans as an employee. Lance had always been aware of other people's opinions, and

I couldn't believe that many of his current associates were the kind of people who supported Ralph Evans.

On the other hand, maybe no one even knew that Lance owned KLWG. Sure, the station's call letters were his initials, but who would think of that? And how many of Lance's associates spent their evenings listening to talk radio?

My thoughts were interrupted by the arrival of the food. The chicken-fried steak was crisp and golden and covered in thick white gravy spotted with black pepper. The Texas toast was heavy with butter. I could feel my cholesterol level rising before I took a bite. The steak was so tender that I could cut it with my fork, and the potatoes had been mashed with the skins on. If I died of a heart attack, I'd die happy. And well fed.

Lindeman seemed to be enjoying his meat loaf as much as I was enjoying my steak. We didn't talk for a while.

When we were finished, Lindeman said that he thought he'd have some of the cherry cobbler. With vanilla ice cream.

I thought that was a fine idea. Life was short, and even in a place like Picketville you might be the victim of a fly-by shooting. You might as well grab all the gusto you could get.

The cobbler was warm, with a thick, doughy crust on the top and the bottom. The ice cream was cold and melted quickly, mixing with the juices of the cobbler. It was even better than the chicken-fried steak.

"Do you eat like this every day?" I asked Lindeman after the cobbler was all gone and the bowls were empty and shining in front of us.

"Just when somebody else is payin'."

"How often is that?"

"Not near often enough."

I wasn't so sure. A steady diet of meals like the one we'd just had and Lindeman would need crutches made of steel. The aluminum ones wouldn't be strong enough to hold him.

"What now?" I asked.

"I don't know about you, but I need a nap. And my leg hurts. I'm gonna take the stuff Dr. Harvey gave me and go to bed. How about you?"

I was going to make a few phone calls, but there was no need to tell Lindeman that.

"I'll take you home and then go back to the motel," I said. "I have to think about what to do next."

"You know what I'd do if I was you?"

"No. You'd better tell me."

"I'd talk to Evans. Tell him you're onto him. Maybe that'll stop him."

"I want to talk to your son first. Maybe I'll go by the station. I can catch Evans there tonight, before his show."

"He won't be by himself."

"I know. I'll be careful."

"Yeah," Lindeman said. "You better."

WHEN LINDA BROUGHT the bill, I asked if I could leave my truck in her parking lot for a while.

"We don't have people towed around here," she said. "This isn't Houston."

"Well, I wouldn't want to take a customer's place."

"I wouldn't want you to, either. Why don't you park around in back, behind the kitchen? There's always a vacant space or two back there."

I thanked her and went out to move the truck. The smell in back of The Toole Shed wasn't nearly as appetizing as the one on the inside, but I didn't let myself think much about it. You can't expect a garbage bin to smell good.

I went back inside and got Lindeman. He was quiet on the drive back to the ranch. When we arrived, he said, "We never did get to see those prairie chickens."

"Some other time," I told him.

I no longer thought the birds very important to what was happening in Picketville. Something else was going on, and I was going to find out what it was. But first I had to talk to Lance again. And to Dino.

"I won't be needin' the truck for a good while, I guess," Lindeman said. "You just use it however you want to."

"If there's any heavy work to be done, I'll get my Chevy."

"That thing couldn't pull a pin out of a pincushion."

I didn't argue with him. I helped him into the house and walked with him to the kitchen, where he took his pills. Then he went into the bedroom.

"I'm just gonna lie down with my clothes on," he said. "I don't think I'll sleep much."

"Depends on what was in those pills," I said.

He grinned. "Doc Harvey wouldn't give me anything too strong."

I told him that we'd find out soon enough, and we did. He was snoring by the time I was out the bedroom door.

13

SINCE LINDEMAN WAS asleep, I could use his telephone and have all the privacy I wanted. I assumed that Lance paid the bill, so Lindeman wouldn't be out any money. I didn't want to call from the Picketville Inn. There was no need to tempt the switchboard operator to listen in.

My first call was to Lance. He was still in a meeting, or so the secretary said, and she refused to call him to the telephone. I tried the "it's an emergency" bit on her again, and this time it worked. Sort of. She said that Mr. Garrison had heard about "the trouble" and would call me back. I didn't really believe her. When a big-time executive was "in a meeting," he never called you back. But I didn't have anything better to do, so I gave her the number and hung up.

I wondered who had told Lance about what had happened. Obviously it was someone with a lot more pull than me. Then the phone rang. I was surprised to hear Lance's voice when I answered.

"What's this I hear about somebody shooting at you from an airplane?" he said.

I told him the story and said, "I didn't come here to be shot at."

"I know. And believe me, I didn't think anything like that would happen. I don't know—" He was interrupted by a loud shrieking noise. "Damn office chair. I'm going to get a new one as soon as I have time. Look, Tru, don't worry about this. It's bound to be some kind of crazy stunt that doesn't mean anything. I'll drive out there tomorrow and see if I can help you figure out what's happening."

I told him that I didn't need help so much as I needed to know more about prairie chickens. "They must be really valuable birds if someone wants to shoot me to keep me from even looking at them."

"They aren't valuable at all, not to anyone except a few environmentalists. Give me some time to think about this. We'll talk tomorrow."

He broke the connection before I had a chance to say anything else. It wasn't exactly a satisfactory conversation, but I'd try to pin him down to something specific when I saw him. That is, I'd try if he actually showed up.

My next call was to Dino. There wasn't much doubt that he would be at home, and he was.

"I'm watching this guy who's written some books about all kinds of miracle drugs that the stupid FDA won't let us buy," he said when I asked what he was up to. "But you can get them in Mexico and Europe."

"What kind of drugs?" I asked.

"The kind that make you feel better and live longer. I'm gonna order those books."

He didn't add "as soon as you get off the phone," but I knew he was thinking it.

"What about my cat?" I asked.

"That cat's crazy about me," he said. "Rubbed against my leg and everything when I went out there to feed him this morning. He wanted me to scratch his back, but I didn't have time."

"You're just trying to make me jealous."

"Hey, not me. Can I help it if I'm irresistible?"

"I guess not. Don't forget to go out again late this afternoon."

"What? You have to tell me? Don't you trust me?"

"Trust doesn't have a thing to do with it. I'm just reminding you because Nameless likes things to run according to schedule. Otherwise, he gets nervous. And I have a couple of other favors to ask."

"I figured. You wouldn't be calling just to find out about that cat. So what's happening?"

I gave him the short version, and he said, "Sounds pretty damned fishy to me. I think Lance is giving you the old screw job."

"So do I, but so far I haven't figured out exactly how or why. I think you were right about his nose. He still remembers."

"Some people like to let things sit for a while before they get revenge. There's a saying about it."

" 'Revenge is a dish best served cold,' " I said.

"Yeah, something like that. What else did you want?"

"I want you to use some of your contacts to find out about this Ralph Evans. I need anything you can come up with. And check on Lance, too, while you're at it. He seems to own about half of Picketville."

"Anything else?"

"That should do it for now. I'll be in touch."

"I figured."

"Tell Evelyn hello for me."

He said he would and hung up. Then I called Johnny Bates, who also didn't get out much. He answered on the first ring and said he'd be glad to find whatever he could on Ralph Evans and Lance Garrison.

"Those rich guys, though, they're tough, Tru. Boxes in boxes in boxes, you know what I mean?"

I knew. "Just get what you can. I'll call you tomorrow."

"Right. I'll be here."

I hung up feeling a little better. I'd been shot at, but I'd been able to run up Lance's long-distance phone bill. There was some small satisfaction in that.

I looked in the bedroom to check on Lindeman, though there was no need. I could hear him snoring all the way from the living room. He was fine, so I left him there and went back to Picketville.

STATION KLWG WASN'T exactly imposing. It was housed in a little cinder-block building not far from the downtown area. It was painted a bluish gray and surrounded by an untrimmed hedge. The lawn hadn't been mowed in a while, either.

I parked Lindeman's Dodge and went inside the building. There was a large lobby, but there was no receptionist at the desk. Metal folding chairs stood all around the walls, and there were standing ashtrays near most of them. KLWG didn't have a "No Smoking" policy. I saw a gray door with STATION MANAGER painted on it in black letters, so I walked over and knocked.

A man called out for me to come on in, so I did. He was sitting at a desk covered with papers and notebooks, and he was writing something on a yellow legal pad. A speaker on the wall was playing a Rush Limbaugh clone, but the volume was turned very low, for which I was grateful.

"Be with you in a second," the man at the desk said. "Have a seat."

I sat in a chair that was even more uncomfortable than the ones in the doctor's office and watched the man write.

He had a square face and thick gray hair that had a slight wave in it. He wore a white shirt, no coat, and a striped tie.

And he was wearing a pair of half glasses, which meant he was probably farsighted. He looked older than Anne, and the glasses cinched it. Anne and I hadn't quite reached the age at which we were having to hold things at arm's length to focus on them.

When he stopped writing, he looked at me over the tops of the glasses.

"What can I do for you?" he asked.

"I'm Truman Smith. Lance Garrison probably called you about me."

He stood up and extended his hand across the desk. I stood and shook it. Unlike Martin York, he didn't try to prove anything.

"I'm Paul Lindeman," he said when we'd shaken hands and seated ourselves again. "Lance called, like you said, and I've heard a lot about you from Anne."

"All of it good, I hope."

"Oh, sure. She said you were quite a football player in high school and that now you're a private eye."

"Just like on TV," I said.

He shook his head. "I don't think so. I don't remember Magnum ever having a case that involved a dead bird."

"It's more than a bird," I told him, and then went on to tell him briefly what had happened that afternoon.

He interrupted only once, leaning forward tensely. "Is my father all right?"

"He's fine. There's no serious damage, and he'll be walking without the crutches before long."

My answer seemed to relax him, and he told me to go on. When I was finished, he said, "Do you think Ralph Evans could have been behind it?"

"Your father does. I don't know what to think. Tell me about Evans."

Paul looked uncomfortable. "What do you want to know?"

"I've heard that you don't get along with him."

"He's been good for the station. He's brought in a lot of advertisers."

It was a canned answer. It sounded good, and it was probably loyal, but it didn't have anything to do with the question.

"That's not what I asked about," I said.

Lindeman sat a little straighter in his chair. "All right. Evans and I don't like each other." He indicated the speaker. "I can listen to Rush Limbaugh and some of the others like him, but I think Evans's views are a little extreme, and I don't think he's good for the station. He's well aware that I feel that way."

"What about Lance? Does he like Evans?"

Lindeman looked up at the ceiling, then down at the floor. He seemed to be more uncomfortable with the idea of talking about Lance than with the idea of discussing Evans.

Finally he said, "Lance likes the advertising. That's all he cares about—the money. But I've been looking into that."

"What do you mean?"

He didn't answer for a second or two, as if he'd made some kind of slip. Then he said, "Sponsors have been dropping off the show. The big names. We still sell some local spots, but the Houston advertisers are leaving us."

"What does Lance think about that?"

"I haven't really presented the figures to him yet. In fact, that's what I was working on when you came in."

He smiled for the first time since I'd entered the room and leaned back in his chair.

"You must like what you've come up with," I said.

"I guess it won't hurt to tell you. We've been losing revenue for the last month on Evans's show. We haven't been able to fill all the spots, and we're using a lot of public service announcements."

"So you might have a good reason to pull the plug on him?"

"Maybe. I'll have to talk to Lance first. He's the owner; I'm just the hired help."

He said the last sentence with something like bitterness. I probably wouldn't have liked working full-time for Lance, either. I wasn't exactly ecstatic to be working for him for even a day or so.

Anyway, Lance might be glad to hear Paul's news. It wouldn't matter then who'd killed the prairie chicken. Lance would have a reason to fire Evans. Maybe I could even go home.

"What about Evans?" I asked. "Does he know what's going on?"

"He has a pretty good idea. He tried to talk to me about it earlier today, but I didn't have time for him. I'm sure he'll get back to me. He seemed pretty worried about it."

"When was that?"

"When? Early this morning. Why?"

"No reason. Did he get violent?"

Paul sat up straight again. "No. He leaves that to Gar and Bert."

The thought of Gar and Bert didn't seem to make him very happy. It didn't make me happy, either.

"That might have been them in the plane," he said. "I think Bert can fly. Anyway, even if you don't know who did it, I can get the story on the air. It's news, and KLWG will be the first with the story. I'll get Tony in here. We don't have any real newspeople anyhow, but Tony does some reporting for us. Would you give him an exclusive interview?"

"No interviews. Tell me about your run-in with Evans this morning."

"It wasn't much of a run-in. He just said that he knew what I was up to, and that I wasn't going to get away with it. He said he'd see me later."

"And do you think he will?"

"Who knows? He's crazy. You never know what a crazy man will do."

That made two people who thought Evans was crazy. I didn't think so, but I was beginning to wonder. Maybe they were right and I was wrong.

"If he's tied to the dead bird, not even Lance can save him," Paul said. "I hope you find out that he did it, or had it done."

"Do you think he might have?"

"It's the kind of thing he might do, sort of a symbolic gesture, you might say."

What was the use of a gesture if you didn't take the credit for it? Evans didn't seem like the shy type.

I stood up. "I'd like to meet Evans. What time does he get here to do his show?"

"He likes to come in early. He'll probably be here by six-thirty. But he'll have his crowd with him."

"Bert and Gar?"

"Them, too. But he has a regular entourage. You'll see."

"You won't be here?"

"No. I don't put in a twenty-four-hour day, at least not every day. But the station will be open."

"All right. Say hello to Anne for me."

He looked at his desk. "I'll do that."

Then he stood up and put out his hand again. I shook it and turned to go.

"Do you carry a gun?" he asked.

I turned back. "No. Should I?"

"Probably not, but watch yourself around Evans and his crew. They do."

"That's a real comfort," I said.

Paul smiled, and it made him look a little younger. "Glad I could brighten your day."

14

I DROVE TO the Picketville Inn and lay on the bed to think things over.

Lance had asked me to come to town and investigate the death of his endangered species bird, but so far I hadn't come up with a single clue.

The fact that I was clueless didn't seem to matter, however, because someone obviously didn't like the fact that I was poking around. Either that or someone had it in for Red Lindeman, and he didn't seem to think that was a possibility.

Everyone seemed to suspect Ralph Evans of having killed the prairie chicken, but there was no proof that he'd been anywhere near the bird. Certainly no one had seen him. Red Lindeman thought Evans had taken the shots at us from the plane, too, but there was no proof of that, either.

All in all, it hadn't been a very productive day. I'd had a good chicken-fried steak, however. That was worth something, though I'm not sure it was worth getting shot at. I couldn't make up my mind about that point, and after a few minutes my mind began to drift and then I went to sleep.

THIS TIME I didn't dream about birds. I dreamed that Anne came by to see me at the Picketville Inn. She looked young, as young as she had in high school, and she told me that she was going to leave her husband because life with him was tedious and boring. She wanted a more exciting life, the kind of life that being married to a big-time private eye could give her.

I was just about to accept her proposal when someone knocked on the door and woke me.

I sat up and looked around the room, trying to figure out exactly where I was. My mouth was dry, and I had to swallow twice before I could say, "Just a second."

I went into the bathroom and ran some water from the faucet into the flimsy plastic glass that the Inn provided. I took a couple of swallows, and my mouth felt better. Then I went to the door and looked through the viewer. Anne was standing outside, waiting patiently.

I'd never had a dream come true before. I wondered if this would be the first time, but somehow I doubted it. I opened the door, trying to look the way I imagined a big-time private eye would look.

"Hi," Anne said, and smiled.

I remembered that smile all too well, but I got only a minor slug from the guy with the sledge. Nothing at all, really, compared to the hammering I'd gotten while running across the marsh earlier that day. But then that might have been the binoculars.

"What brings you here?" I asked Anne.

"I was in the neighborhood and thought I'd stop by," she said. "How's that for a corny opening line? Are you going to ask me in?"

I stepped back and to the side. "Sure. It's not exactly the Ritz, though."

"I know." She walked past me and into the room. "The Inn has been here longer than I have."

"I could tell. You can have the chair. I'll sit on the floor."

Considering the dream I'd just had, I thought it might be a little out of line to suggest that either of us sit on the bed.

She looked around the room before sitting down. She didn't seem impressed.

"I've never been inside one of these rooms before," she said.

"You have a home here," I said.

"But maybe not for long." She sat down. "I'm trying to talk Paul into leaving."

"Why?"

"Because he never has time for anything except his job. He needs to get away from that radio station. He spends all his time there, and I don't think it's good for him."

I guess she wasn't planning to ask me to take her away from Picketville and make her a part of my exciting life after all. I eased myself down to the floor, trying to keep my bones from creaking, and leaned against the wall.

"Do you worry about Paul a lot?" I asked.

"All the time. I care so much for him, and he's working himself to death. And then there's Ralph Evans."

"Evans isn't much of a threat, is he?"

"How can you say that after what happened today?"

"You know about that?"

"Everybody in town knows about that. It was on the KLWG news at five o'clock, but people were talking about it long before then. I called Red as soon as I heard, but there was no answer. I called back a little while ago, and he said he was fine. He said you were OK, too."

"This town doesn't need a local news broadcast much, does it?"

She smiled. "Not really, but it makes everyone feel good

to have the gossip confirmed by official sources. Do you think Evans was behind the shooting?"

"I don't know. The sheriff is supposed to be investigating that end of things."

"I'm sure. But not too hard, I'll bet. He and Evans are good friends."

"Then he should be working to clear his friend."

"Oh, he'll clear him, all right. Probably by tomorrow. You should stay away from Sheriff Peavy if you can. He's a dangerous man."

"Why do you say that?"

"Paul's having someone at the station look into things that happened at the jail."

"Like what?"

She hesitated as if she wished she hadn't mentioned it, but then she said, "You might have heard the story of the prisoner who hanged himself a few months ago. Or he was supposed to have hanged himself. There was a rumor going around that said he had a lot of help. Sheriff Peavy headed up an internal investigation, and the department came out with clean hands. But Paul says there might be a lot more to the story."

I hadn't heard anything about that incident, but it was one more thing for me to think about. Peavy didn't look like the kind of man who would appreciate having someone poke in his business.

"Does the sheriff know about the investigation?" I asked.

"Oh, he knows, all right. He knows a little about everything that happens in this county."

"So how does he feel about it?"

"He doesn't like it a bit. Paul has had several anonymous calls telling him that it would be better for him if he called off the investigation."

"Were the calls from Peavy?"

"Probably not. If they were, he was disguising his voice. But he's behind them. I don't have any doubt of that."

"What about Martin York?" I asked.

"Martin? What do you mean?"

"How does he fit into all this, aside from the fact that he's a birder?"

"Well, of course he probably knows as much about prairie chickens as anyone, and he's done a lot to help Red with the ranch. He and the Greers are about the only people that Lance gives free access to the ranch."

I thought that was interesting. Whoever killed the bird had to know where to find it, and from what I'd learned so far, the birds were pretty shy. It wouldn't be easy just to drive out to the ranch and shoot one.

"York seems to like you quite a bit," I said.

Anne laughed. "You noticed? Well, I suppose it's obvious. Martin could become a bit of a problem, I think."

"How?"

"He's a little too aggressive. I can handle him, but he can be a real pest."

I knew I hadn't liked Martin for some reason, and now I liked him a whole lot less.

"Do you want to give me any details?"

"Not really. He seems to think that I should leave Paul and go away with him. He has some idea about traveling around the world, looking for birds."

Apparently York was having the same kind of dreams I was, but he was more willing to act his out.

"What does your husband think about that?"

"He doesn't know, and I'm not going to tell him. He might do something he'd regret. I can handle Martin."

That was the second time she'd said that. I wondered if she was trying to convince me or herself.

"Maybe I should have a little talk with him," I said.

"You men. Always looking for a chance to flex your muscles. Don't worry about Martin. He's harmless."

Spoken like someone who hadn't shaken hands with Martin York lately. I hoped she knew what she was talking about.

"And then there's Ralph Evans," I said, getting back to our original topic.

"Ralph is a real problem. I think Paul is going to do something about him soon, and I'm a lot more worried about that than about anything Martin might try with me. Martin isn't dangerous, and maybe Ralph isn't either. But he has dangerous friends. I'm afraid of what they might do."

"For example?"

"There have been a few people who disagreed strongly with Ralph and who have made their feelings known. One of them was Bob Greer, and a few nights later his car was run off the road and into a ditch by someone in a black truck. He was lucky that he wasn't seriously hurt."

"Does he know who was driving the truck?"

"He couldn't see. It was too dark, and he was too busy trying to steer his car. He thinks it was Ralph's friends Gar and Bert, but there's no way to be sure. There are a lot of black trucks around here."

It was beginning to appear that Evans was blamed for everything bad that happened in Picketville, or at least he was being blamed by the people I was talking to.

I looked at my watch. It was six forty-five. I said, "I'm going out to the station in a little while to talk to Evans. Do you want to go with me? You can make the introductions."

"Why not? It might be fun."

"Fun" wasn't the word that had occurred to me. "Interesting," maybe, but not fun.

I stood up slowly. It wasn't easy to do without groaning, but I managed it.

"My car or yours?" I asked.

"I saw Red's truck outside. I think my car would be more comfortable."

That was fine with me.

IT DIDN'T TAKE long to get to the station. It didn't take long to get anywhere in Picketville. When we arrived, there were more vehicles in the parking lot than there had been earlier in the day. Most of them were trucks, some of them even more battered than Red's. One of them had more Bondo on it than metal, and a couple of the others were covered with camouflage paint.

"Ralph's army," Anne said. "Or his camp followers. I'm not sure what to call them."

"How about his butt-boys?"

She laughed. I liked to see her laugh. "I think I'll stick to letting Red call them that."

I looked around the parking lot and counted the cars and trucks. There were seven. And there was no way of knowing how many men might have arrived in each one.

"Are you sure you want to go in there?"

Anne got out of her car and leaned her head back inside. "I've seen them before. Come on."

I got out. I wondered if Ralph Evans would talk to me or just have his followers throw me out of the building.

Well, there was one way to find out.

"Can I count on you to protect me?" I asked.

Anne laughed, and we went inside.

15

THERE WERE TEN men sitting in the station lobby. Most of them had cigarettes dangling from their mouths, and the air was thick with gray smoke. The ones who weren't smoking were working on either a dip of snuff or a chaw of tobacco. Maybe they couldn't read the surgeon general's warning, or maybe they just didn't like to take the government's word for anything. Maybe they just didn't care.

Some of them were dressed in combat fatigues, some in camouflage, and some in jeans and work shirts. All of them had on either hats or baseball caps, and all of them looked toward the door when Anne and I entered.

I felt a little like Tom Landry in that old TV ad where he finds himself surrounded by Redskins, so I followed his lead and said, "Heighdy."

They just looked at me, smoke curling upward from their cigarettes.

"Hey, fellas," Anne said. "Where's Ralph?"

"He's back in the greenroom, Miz Lindeman," the man

closest to us said. He didn't bother to remove his cigarette. "Gar and Bert are back there with 'im."

I'd wondered about those two. I'd been hoping they were somewhere else. Thailand, for instance.

"This is Truman Smith," Anne said, nodding toward me. "Paul told him to drop by and talk to Ralph."

The man looked at me the way he might have looked at something particularly nasty he'd discovered on the bottom of his combat boots.

"We know who he is," he said.

"Well, isn't that nice," Anne said. "Come on, Tru. We'll go on back and talk to Ralph. See you boys later."

The man squinted his eyes and waved his hand in front of his face, fanning away the smoke from his cigarette.

"Sure, Miz Lindeman," he said.

As we walked down the hall that led to the green room, conversation in the room started up again. I heard someone ask about the price of Israeli gas masks, and someone else told him where he could get two for less than twenty dollars by mail order.

"They come with one canister a piece," he said. "You got to pay the postage and handling, though."

Not being in the market for a gas mask at the moment, I didn't listen to the rest.

"You know those guys?" I asked Anne.

"I've seen them around the station sometimes when I've come by on days when Paul was working late. They're not so bad. Most of them are farmers, and they think they're getting a raw deal from the government because their taxes are so high. They think Washington should be thinking more about the plight of the American farmer than about what's happening to someone across one of the major oceans. Here's the greenroom."

We were standing in front of a green painted door.

"Cute," I said. "Should I knock?"

"I think so. We don't want to get shot because someone thinks we're ATF agents coming in with a no-knock warrant."

I tapped on the door with my knuckles and a voice that I recognized as belonging to Ralph Evans said that we could come on in. When I opened the door, I saw Evans sitting directly across from me on a couch that might have been brought there right from the Picketville Inn. Bert was to the right of the door with his hand in the pocket of a lightweight nylon jacket. The pocket was bulging with something more than just his hand.

I didn't see Gar, but I knew he was there somewhere, maybe in back of the door.

Evans said, "Come on in, Mr. Smith. You, too, Miz Lindeman."

We walked into the room, and the door swung shut behind us. Sure enough, Gar stood there. He was grinning and showing those wonderful teeth, but there was nothing comical about him.

"I don't think we've been formally introduced," I told Evans.

Evans nodded. "That's the truth. But you know who we are, I'll bet. And we know who you are, don't we, boys?"

"Yeah," Bert said. "We know who you are."

Gar didn't say a thing. He just stood there grinning at me. Maybe he couldn't talk.

"You're the fella who's gonna say we shot that bird," Bert went on. "The one who's gonna say we shot at you and Red from an airplane. That's who you are."

"Now hold on there, Bert," Evans said. "There's no need for us to rush to judgment about what Mr. Smith's going to say about us. Why don't you and Mrs. Lindeman have a seat, Mr. Smith, and we'll have a little talk about this and that."

There were three overstuffed armchairs in the room, all

of them as old as the couch and covered with rips and dark stains. Anne sat in one while I sat in another. Bert and Gar remained standing, never taking their eyes off me. Bert's hand was still in his jacket pocket. I was beginning to think that he didn't trust me.

"Now then, about that prairie chicken," Evans said. "In the first place, I think it's a stupid waste of the public's tax dollars to save some endangered bird, and in the second place, I don't care if somebody killed it. There's thousands of kinds of birds out there. What good's one more kind? Do you think that bird was going to come up with a cure for cancer or invent some kind of supercomputer? No way. Last time I looked, 'birdbrain' wasn't exactly a compliment."

I was beginning to think I was listening to a monologue that Evans had prepared for one of his shows, and I started to interrupt.

Evans didn't let me. "Now hold on. I'll just say my piece and then you can talk. As I was telling you, I don't care if someone killed that bird, but *I* didn't kill it, and neither did Bert or Gar. Did you, boys?"

"Hell, no," Bert said.

Gar didn't say a thing, but when I glanced in his direction he was shaking his head.

"So that settles that," Evans said. "You can say a lot of bad things about me, and come to think of it, people *have* said a lot of bad things about me, but you can't say I'm not a man of my word. If I say I didn't do something, you can take it for the truth, and the same goes for Bert and Gar.

"Now, then, about that airplane. We didn't do that, either. We heard about it, of course, just like everyone else in town heard about it, but that's all. Why, Gar there can't stand airplanes. He gets airsick. Isn't that right, Gar?"

Gar nodded, grinning.

"And Bert? Bert's got a fear of heights. He gets nervous when he climbs a stepladder. Tell him, Bert."

"That's right," Bert said. "I don't even like to stay in a two-story house."

"So that takes care of that," Evans said. "Anything else we can do for you?"

"I wouldn't dream of doubting your word," I said. "And I wouldn't doubt Bert and Gar, either. But let me ask you one thing, just out of curiosity."

"Sure," Evans said. "You go right ahead."

"What were you doing today around noon?"

"I thought you said you believed me."

"I did, but it always helps to have a little verification from another source."

Evans smiled. "I can see that. And I don't mind telling you, either. Just about that time, Bert and Gar and I were having us a hamburger at my house. Bert went to the Burger Barn and picked them up."

So much for verification from another source.

"The girl at the Burger Barn will tell you Bert was there. Right, Bert?"

"Damn straight."

I was sure she would. But I wasn't at all sure that I'd believe her.

"Anything else?" Evans asked, looking satisfied.

"Is it true that Paul Lindeman is going to pull your show as soon as he gets the latest advertising figures together?"

"You son of a bitch," Bert said.

"Now, then, Bert," Evans said, using his smooth radio voice, "just hold on. There's no call for that kind of talk. There's a lady present."

"I don't care about any lady," Bert said. "I'm gonna whip this son of a—"

Evans raised a hand. "Don't say it again, Bert. And you move back where you were, Gar."

Gar was standing right beside me, and I didn't even know how he'd gotten there. I hadn't heard a sound or seen a movement. A chill trickled down my backbone as he backed away.

Evans waited a beat and said, "You can see that the boys don't take kindly to someone who insults me."

"I can see, all right. But that doesn't answer the question."

"I'll answer it, then," Bert said. "Lindeman isn't gonna pull the show. He knows what would happen if he tried."

"No threats, Bert," Evans said. "You know better than that."

Bert didn't look as if he cared.

"And what about Lance Garrison?" I said. "I hear he wouldn't mind getting you off the air."

"That's a damn lie," Bert said. "Garrison loves Ralph's show."

"I've been assured that I have Mr. Garrison's full support," Evans said. "I think I can say with about a hundred percent certainty that he's not going to let the station drop my show. I don't think I have to worry about that."

"The old vote of confidence," I said. "Every losing football coach gets it just before he's canned."

Evans didn't look scared. He just looked bored. "You're wearing out your welcome, Mr. Smith. Why don't you show him out, Gar."

Gar was suddenly beside me again, and this time his hand was on my left elbow, not crushing it, but lifting me straight up out of the chair as if I weighed no more than a dust bunny.

"It's always a pleasure to see you, Mrs. Lindeman," Evans said as Anne stood up. "Give my regards to your husband."

"I'll do that," Anne said. "But I'm not so sure he'll return the thought."

Gar spun me around and propelled me toward the door. I didn't fight it. I was afraid he might do something that I'd regret.

He opened the door with one hand and gave me a light shove in the back with the palm of the other. I didn't quite sail across the hall into the opposite wall, but it took an effort to avoid it.

I heard the door close and turned around. Anne was standing there.

"Friendly bunch of folks you have here in Picketville," I said.

"Don't we, though. Did you learn anything from them?"

"Not much, except that they don't have an alibi for this afternoon. They might have eaten hamburgers for lunch, but that doesn't mean they weren't up in that plane."

"So what's the next step?"

"How are those hamburgers at the Burger Barn?"

"Not quite as hot as the jalapeño burger at The Toole Shed."

"Good. I don't think I'm ready for that yet. Want to join me for dinner?"

She thought about it, but not for long. "Why not? It's been years since we had a date. But only if you spring for French fries, too."

"You've got a deal," I said.

THE BURGER WAS OK, but nothing special. What made things special was the fact that Anne was sitting in the booth across from me, eating French fries with her fingers and drinking Coke through a straw just as she'd done when we were kids.

I was so carried away that I even told a couple of corny jokes, and they made her laugh, or at least she pretended that they did.

When we left the Burger Barn she said, "What are you going to do now?"

It was a nice evening, the full moon breaking through the clouds now and then and just the hint of a breeze. I wanted to go somewhere outside and sit and talk to her, but I didn't know where to go.

"It's such a nice night," Anne said. "There's a roadside park not far from the Inn. You passed it on the way to Lance's ranch this morning. Why don't we go there and talk for a little while?"

Either she still knew me very well or she was feeling the same thing I was, the tug of memory and desire.

"What about Paul?" I said.

"All he thinks about is his job. He won't even miss me. Let's go."

I didn't argue.

THE ROADSIDE PARK wasn't a big one. There were two concrete tables with concrete benches and a litter barrel shaded by spreading oak trees that had no doubt been planted by the highway department sixty or seventy years previously.

We sat on one of the benches and talked for over an hour—about the good times we'd had in Galveston so many years before, and about the things that had happened since.

Anne went first. As it turned out, she hadn't traveled much more of the world than I had, but she said that life in Picketville wasn't all bad, and she didn't beg me to take her away with me.

"I get away from Picketville now and then," she said. "I go to Houston, and I visit Galveston. There's plenty to keep me busy. And Paul's a good man, maybe better than I deserve. I worry about him."

"Why?" I asked.

"You heard what Bert Ware said. He and Gar are violent men. Both of them have been arrested more than once for brawling, but Evans always makes their bond."

"Do you think they killed the prairie chicken?"

"I don't think it would bother either one of them to kill a prairie chicken. Or a human being, for that matter."

I didn't think so either, but I didn't want to talk about Bert and Gar. Anne asked why I'd gone back to Galveston, and I told her a little about Jan. Not much. I wasn't sure that I knew the whole story, and I didn't want to blacken anyone's memory without being certain.

She moved a little closer to me and said, "That's terrible. I know you must feel really sad about it."

She brushed my shoulder with her own, and I felt seventeen again. I thought for maybe a tenth of a second about slipping my arm around her the way I had in the Broadway theater on our first date, but then she smiled, stood up, and said it was time for her to go.

She took me back to the Picketville Inn, where I took a very cold shower, read a couple of chapters from *Tobacco Road*, and went to bed.

I slept without dreaming until 4:39 A.M. I know the exact time because there was a digital clock radio on the nightstand. Its glowing red numbers were the first thing I saw when Sheriff Peavy and his deputy came through the door and dragged me out of bed.

They told me that Paul Lindeman was dead, and that they were pretty sure who'd killed him.

Me.

16

DEPUTY DENBOW STOOD in front of the door with his arms crossed over his chest. If anything, his eyes were redder than they'd been that afternoon.

I was sitting on the edge of the bed in my Jockey shorts and T-shirt, trying to get my sleep-muddled mind in gear, while Sheriff Peavy hulked over me as if he hoped I'd make some kind of move that would allow him to club me in the head with the short-barreled .38 Special that his jacket had been pulled back to reveal.

If I'd been a desperate criminal, I might have made a grab for it and tried to shoot him. Since I wasn't desperate, at least not yet, I was careful not to make any move at all.

"What makes you think I killed Paul Lindeman?" I asked.

The inside of my mouth tasted worse than it had that afternoon, as if the Chinese Nationalist Army had marched through it wearing unwashed sweat socks, but I didn't think it would be a good idea to ask if I could get a drink. And I was sure that Peavy wouldn't let me get one even if I did ask.

"Because you were out with his wife tonight," Denbow

said from the door. "That's what makes us think you killed him. We know all about it."

"We just ate a hamburger and talked," I said. "That's all."

Denbow shook his head as if sadly disappointed in me. "That's not what we hear."

"Who did you talk to?" I asked, though I had a pretty good idea. Thank you, Ralph Evans.

Denbow walked over to the bed and stood beside Peavy. "That's none of your business."

He poked me in the chest with a stiffened index finger. I was already bruised from the binoculars, but I didn't flinch. Well, I didn't flinch much.

"And don't ask any more questions," he said. "That's our job."

"Where was he killed?" I asked, just to show him he couldn't scare me.

"You should know," Peavy said. "Since you did it. Why don't you tell us?"

"Because I *don't* know. I'm trying to find out."

"You know, all right," Denbow said. He grabbed a handful of my T-shirt and yanked me off the bed and onto my knees. "You made the phone call."

I jerked backward, pulling the shirt from his hand. I pushed away from him and stood up.

"Don't do that," I said, and he swung his right fist at my head.

I ducked aside and started to sink a good hard right about three inches into his stomach, but I was stopped by Peavy's .38 against my temple.

"Why don't you just sit back on the bed and cool off," he said.

The cold barrel of the .38 had a soothing effect on my temper, and I sat down.

"Keep your deputy away from me," I said. I was breathing a little heavily, but I said it calmly.

Peavy didn't even bother to glance at Denbow, who was standing a few feet away looking as if he'd like to do a little work on my face with his baton.

Peavy said, "Paul Lindeman was shot about two hours ago, outside the radio station. His wife told us that someone had called him and told him there was an emergency there. He didn't tell her what it was. He just said he'd be back in about an hour. When he didn't come back in two hours, she called the station. There was no answer, and that's when she called us. We went over to the station and found Lindeman lying by his car. Somebody used a twelve-gauge shotgun on him. There wasn't much left of his head."

Something twisted in my stomach. I'd liked Paul Lindeman, enough to be the least bit ashamed that I was attracted to his wife, and now he was dead. It wasn't my fault, but I still felt a little guilty.

"I never met Lindeman before yesterday," I said. "I knew his wife years ago, but we haven't seen each other since high school. We had a hamburger tonight at the Burger Barn and then talked for a while at a roadside park, but that's all there was to it—talk. You can ask her."

Peavy looked over his shoulder at Denbow. Denbow shrugged.

Peavy turned back to me. "We did ask her. She tells the same story. But she would."

"This is ridiculous." I started to get up, but Peavy wiggled the .38 and I stayed seated. "You know I didn't kill anyone."

"Do you have a shotgun?" Denbow asked.

"Of course not. I don't have any gun at all."

"Then you won't mind if we search your truck."

"I wouldn't mind, but it's not here. It's out at the Garrison place. I'm driving Red Lindeman's truck."

I wondered if anyone had told Red about his son. I was glad it wasn't my job to do it.

"I saw Red's truck outside," Peavy said. "We'll just search that one."

"Not without me," I told him.

I wasn't going to let them plant a shotgun in the truck while I sat in the motel room. I pulled on my jeans and we went outside into the humid early-morning air. The blue glow of a mercury vapor lamp floated over us. I hadn't bothered to lock the truck, so I told Denbow to go ahead and look inside.

He opened the door and pulled back the seat. There was nothing there except what you might expect: a tow chain, a hammer, a set of cheap socket wrenches, a pair of work gloves, and some oily rags.

"No shotgun," Denbow said to Peavy, slamming the seat back into place. "But that doesn't mean he didn't do it."

"That prairie chicken of Garrison's was killed with a twelve gauge," I said. "I wasn't anywhere near here when that happened."

"That doesn't prove diddly," Denbow said. "There's no way to show that the same two guns were used, not with shotguns."

"It's something to think about, though," I said. "I'm surprised that it hadn't occurred to you."

"Oh, it occurred to us," Peavy said. "We may be country boys, Mr. Smith, but we're not stupid."

He didn't look stupid. In the ghostly light of the parking lot, he looked both tough and sly.

"If I were you, I'd look for someone with a grudge against Lindeman," I said. "Not some stranger in town."

"Wiseass," Denbow said, but he didn't really seem to mean it.

"We're going to let you go for now," Peavy said. "But I hope you were planning to stick around town for a few days."

"You couldn't pay me to leave," I said.

They weren't amused, but they'd had their fun with me and it was time for them to go. They both looked disappointed, as if they'd thought I'd confess and make their job easy. Or maybe they were just sorry that I hadn't given them a chance to shoot me.

I watched them get into their patrol car and leave. Denbow was driving, and he took off fast, spraying gravel from beneath the back wheels just to impress me. When they were out of sight, I went back inside to shave and finish dressing.

ANNE LIVED IN a red brick house with a neat yard and white wooden shutters on the windows. Red was with her in the living room when I arrived. There were a few friends there, too, and I was introduced to all of them, but I didn't try to remember their names.

And then there was Martin York, wearing a dark suit and a white shirt with a black tie. I thought he was showing far too much attention to Anne, taking every opportunity to hold her hand or to put his arm across her shoulders. He was trying to look bereaved, but I thought he just looked hopeful.

Anne was calm and dry-eyed, which I took as a bad sign. I didn't know much about grief, but I knew that it was best not to keep it all inside. I'd tried that, and it hadn't worked very well.

After I'd told her the things most people do in similar situations, about how sorry I was and how I'd do whatever I could to help, Red motioned for me to follow him into the kitchen. He wasn't wearing a suit; he didn't even have on a tie. I wondered why. Maybe because of his leg wound; he was still using the crutches.

When we got to the kitchen, I saw that friends and neighbors had brought in quite a bit of food. I could smell apple pie, and there was a chocolate cake on the table. A couple of casserole dishes sat on the stove.

Red leaned against the counter and said, "You know who killed him, don't you?"

"No."

"Ralph Evans," Red said. His voice almost cracked with emotion, but he kept it under control. Real men don't cry. "Ralph killed that bird, and now he's killed Paul. Paul never hurt him, any more than the bird did."

"You don't know that Evans killed him," I said. "You might want it to be that way, but you don't know."

"He killed that bird, and he tried to kill Bob Greer. Did you hear about that?"

I said that I had. "But there's no proof of any of those things. If Evans killed Paul, I want to know about it as much as you do. But we have to have some kind of proof."

"What if we could find that airplane?"

"That might help."

"I thought so. I got an idea about where it might be. We can go up there right now."

Now I knew why he wasn't wearing a suit.

"Anne needs you here," I said, thinking that she might even need protection from York. "I can go. You tell me where."

"You don't know your way around this part of the country I'll have to show you."

He needed something to do. Some people are like that. Others just sit and stare, like Anne.

"What about the sheriff?" I asked. "Shouldn't we tell him what you suspect and let him check it out?"

Red wasn't impressed with that idea. "If the plane were in some other county, that might be a good idea. But it's in this county, and Sheriff Peavy and Evans are too buddy-buddy for us to tell Peavy anything right now. If we told him, he might check it out, or he might not. But if he did, he'd let Evans know where he was goin'. By the time he got there, the plane would be long gone. If we find it, then we'll have proof. That'll be time enough to let the sheriff know. Now, are we goin' to find that plane, or not?"

"Later, maybe," I said. "I have to make a few phone calls first. You can stay here with Anne until I get back."

He didn't like it, but he agreed. I went to look for a telephone.

THE DAY WAS warm and the air was thick with humidity. Dark clouds were gathering in the north, and a breeze was rustling in the leaves of the trees. I knew it would probably rain before noon.

I found a pay phone at a convenience store near The Toole Shed. There was no privacy, and I wished for the days of the phone booth. What I had was a telephone with two blue elephant ears sticking out from the wall on either side of it. There was no one around to listen, however, so it really didn't matter.

I dropped a quarter into the slot, and at the tone I got my quarter back and punched in my calling-card number.

"The cat's fine," Dino said after his initial greeting. "Loves me like a brother. I sat in your lawn chair and rubbed him for a while. I'm pretty sure he wants to leave you and move in with me."

"I could sue you," I said. "Alienation of affection."

"Yeah, there's that, but you wouldn't sue an old buddy, would you?"

"Only if I could find a lawyer to take the case."

"You could probably find twenty if you went to the courthouse, so I guess I'll let you keep the cat. But you probably didn't really want to hear about him, anyway. You want me to tell you about Lance Garrison and Ralph Evans."

"That would be nice."

He didn't waste any more words. From what he'd been able to find out, Evans was exactly what he seemed to be, a radio talk-show host with a pretty good following and a man who was deeply suspicious of the federal government. But the following was dwindling, as Lindeman had implied. There were even a few people in Houston who were trying to organize a boycott of his show's advertisers. So it was no wonder that the radio station's revenue was dropping off.

"What about Lance?" I asked.

"Well, now. Old Lance. Seems he's made a few mistakes himself. I guess he thought the market could never let him down. But now that everyone else is getting rich, he's not doing so well. He's taken some chances that haven't paid off so well."

"But he still owns half the town here, right?"

"And a lot more, so I hear. Nothing on paper, though. He's probably still set, financially. There's just one little problem."

"What's that?"

"There's a rumor that the IRS has taken an interest in him. There's supposed to have been an investigation into the legality of some of his investments. If that's true, he's got big trouble."

Dino wasn't exactly a fan of the IRS's. On that topic, he would probably have agreed with Ralph Evans. I told him to be good to the cat and hung up.

Johnny Bates had some news of his own. With just a computer and a modem, he can do things with your bank account that you don't even want to know about.

"Evans is broke," he said. "I don't know what he spends his money on, but it goes pretty fast. There's one really big payment every month, and by the end of the month, he doesn't have any more in his account than you do."

"How do you know about my account?"

"Hey, relax. It was just a guess. And your old buddy Garrison has been in a little trouble, too. He's having a cash-flow problem, but nothing too bad."

"What about his holdings around Picketville?" I asked.

"Hard to say. Boxes in boxes, like I told you. A lot of it's in corporations, but he's probably behind them. His big trouble is with Uncle Sam."

"Internal Revenue?"

"Good guess. This is just a rumor I came up with; it's not solid. Word is, he got involved in some questionable tax shelters in the good old 1980s, and Uncle has come down hard on them. It looks like Garrison's going to get stuck for a bundle. I could find out for sure if you really need the information."

I could tell he wanted to do the digging. It was what he enjoyed more than anything, and I knew he'd love to try hacking into the IRS computers, if he hadn't done it already. But I didn't think it was that important.

"I'll let you know," I told him. "I think you've done enough for now."

"Sure." He sounded disappointed. "I'll send you a bill."

"You do that. And don't undercharge. Lance Garrison will be paying."

"If he can afford it," Johnny said, and I told him I'd call if I needed anything else. Then I drove back to Anne's house to pick up Red Lindeman.

17

W H E N I G O T back to Anne's, Lance had arrived. He had on a suit that probably cost five times what Martin York's had, and he was even more solicitous than York had been. I had to fight the urge to break his nose again.

He took me aside for a private talk and told me how terrible it was that Paul had been killed. "And you getting shot at from that plane. I just don't understand what's going on."

"That makes two of us," I told him.

"Red tells me that you think Ralph Evans may be involved."

"It's just something I'm checking on."

"It's possible, I suppose. Ralph is on shaky ground at the station, and he's not the kind of man who likes to lose."

"Can he fly a plane?"

"I don't know about that. Are you looking for the plane?"

"Red thinks he knows where it might be. We're going to see what we can find."

"Do you want me to go with you?"

I didn't want Lance in my way, no matter what happened, so I shook my head. "I don't think we'll need any help. You can stay here with Anne. She's the one who needs support."

He didn't disagree. I went to find Red, and we left.

THE PLACE WHERE Red wanted us to go wasn't far away. It was up near Columbus, just off Interstate 10. We headed in that direction, with the clouds thickening overhead.

"Evans has got himself a lot of land up there," Red said. "He and some of his buddies use it for camping out and playing soldier. They're all gonna move up there and hold out when the government comes after 'em and tries to put 'em in the concentration camps. That's where the plane's gonna be."

We were in my truck. I wasn't sure that Red's would have stood up to the trip. We were also armed. We'd gone out to Lance's and picked up a couple of pistols that Red said were "for home defense."

He'd let me have a Smith & Wesson Chief's Special with a two-inch barrel, and he was carrying a Model 66, the "Combat Magnum," with a six-inch barrel. You could defend a pretty big home with one of those. You could defend a small town with one.

While we drove, Red talked about his son.

"Paul always loved this part of the country," he said. "He was glad when we sold the farm, because it was a lot of work with not much return, and I was gettin' too old to be of much help to him. We both knew Mr. Garrison, and he was glad to give us jobs. Paul took to the work at the station like a duck to water. He was worried about Ralph Evans, though, thought he'd be trouble, and he sure enough was."

He looked out the window and didn't say anything for a while. His crutches were between us, leaning against the seat.

More to be making conversation than anything else, I said, "What about the man who hanged himself at the jail? Was Paul investigating that?"

Red turned away from the window. "Who told you about that?"

"Anne."

He nodded. "She's a fine woman. Paul was lucky to have met her." He was quiet again. Then he said, "Anyway, about that man at the jail. He was just some fella who'd been in town for a few days. He got drunk somewhere and started some trouble, then got arrested. They say he tore up his shirt and used that and his pants. Hung himself from the bars on the window. The sheriff said that's all there was to it, but Paul wasn't sure."

"Why not?"

"There was something funny about the man. People came snoopin' around after he was dead, but they never told anybody who they were or what they were after, at least not that I heard about. Maybe Paul found out something more, and I think he did. He sure seemed bothered by the whole thing, but he didn't tell me much about it. And he didn't usually do much investigatin' himself. If there was any story, it was likely Tony who went after it. That's Tony Lopez, at the station. He's about the only reporter at the station, and he usually covers stolen dogs and things like that."

We were getting beyond the flat prairie now. There were trees showing up, and even a few hills. It wasn't nearly as woodsy as Fred Benton's place, but it seemed to me to have a little more character than the area around Picketville.

"Do you see Fred Benton often?" I asked.

"Haven't seen that old cuss in years, but I read all about that alligator business in the paper. You did a good job over there."

There was more to the story than the newspapers had

ever printed, but I didn't feel like going into it. I said, "What about this place we're going to now? How did you find out about it?"

"Ever'body knows about it, but I'd forgot it till Lance mentioned it this mornin'. Evans talks about it on his show all the time, but I don't hardly ever listen to him. It's got a lot of trees and some lakes. Lots of places to hide out and play war with those Minute Men of his. It covers a lot of ground."

I thought I knew now where Evans's money was going. Unless he had some income other than what he got from his radio show, he must be sinking everything he had into the property we were about to visit.

"How are we supposed to get on this place?" I asked.

If Evans was as paranoid as I suspected, he might even have armed guards stationed somewhere.

"Won't be a problem," Lindeman said. "We'll find a way."

I wasn't quite so confident, but it turned out that he was right. We turned off the highway and drove down a paved county road for a couple of miles until we came to an area that looked like something out of a World War II movie. There were high banks of earth piled at random and covered with weeds and scrawny willow trees. There were pools of water that didn't qualify as lakes scattered here and there; they didn't look as if they were the work of any natural process.

I slowed down. "What happened here?"

"Damned if I know," Red said. "Looks like there was a lot of blasting at one time or another. Makes a good place to practice your sneak attacks, though, don't it?"

"This is Evans's property?"

"Bound to be. Looks just the way Lance said it did. Now all we got to do is find a way in."

We drove down the road for about a quarter of a mile before we came to a gate. It was a very sturdy gate, made of welded iron bars, and it was held to the fence by a thick chain that was fastened together at the ends with a heavy padlock. There was no armed guard, however.

"So what do you think?" I asked.

"We could call Evans and ask him to give us his permission to visit."

"Somehow I don't think that would be a good idea."

"I guess we could pick that lock, then. You want to do it, or you want me to?"

I thought he was joking, but he wasn't. He reached into his pants' pocket and brought out a set of lock picks.

"I thought you private eyes all had stuff like this," he said, holding up the picks. There were five of them dangling from a gold key chain. "I gotta admit I heard about these things on one of Evans's shows, and then I went out and bought one of those survival magazines and saw the ad for 'em. Cost around fifteen dollars, includin' the postage. They're real good for openin' padlocks."

There was just one thing I wanted to know. "Why did you need them? You don't make a habit of opening other people's gates, do you?"

"Nope. But there're a lot of gates on Lance's place, and sometimes the keys get lost. I keep these things in a drawer where I can find 'em."

"Have you ever used them?"

"Once. Worked just fine. You watch me and you might learn something."

I helped him get out of the truck and crutch his way over to the gate. The wind was picking up, shaking the tall grass in the ditch that ran beside Evans's property. I held up the lock while Red balanced himself and slid in one of the picks. He was right; it worked just fine. There was a satisfactory click, and the lock popped open.

We got back in the truck and drove through the gate. I

stopped on the other side and got out to put the chain back in place.

"Put the lock back in the links," Red told me, "but don't snap it shut."

I wasn't quite that dumb. I arranged the lock so that it would appear from the road to be clasped and got back in the truck.

"Now what?" I said.

"Now we look for that airplane."

WE FOLLOWED A dirt road that wound among the pools and mounds of earth. We could see a long line of trees some distance away, and when we drove around the last of the mounds we saw something else.

Between us and the trees there was a long, open stretch of ground covered with short, dry grass. The wind chased cloud shadows across it, and I could see that it would make a pretty good runway. It would be easy for a skilled pilot to land a plane there.

And maybe someone had. Near the tree line there was a large sheet-metal building with a sliding door in front. It looked almost like an airplane hangar.

"It's in there," Red said. "I know it is."

I wasn't so sure, but it seemed like a good possibility that he was right.

Not far from the hangar there was a small house that looked as if it had been built by novice carpenters. It probably had no more than two rooms, and I supposed it was used as Evans's headquarters when he and his minions came to camp out. A GI-green truck was parked beside the house. I asked Red if he recognized the truck.

"Looks a little like the one that fella Gar drives. Could be his."

If Gar was there, there might be others, though I was afraid Gar alone would be enough to cause us plenty of trouble.

"I'm going to drive a little closer," I said. "We need to get a look in that building to see if the plane's really in there."

Red was already convinced. "It's in there, all right. It's bound to be. But I wouldn't drive any closer if I was you. If you do that, whoever's in that house is goin' to spot us. I'd just as soon that didn't happen."

He might not be right about the plane, but he was right about that. I said, "Why don't I back up and park behind one of those hills? Then I'll go take a look, just to be sure the plane's really there. You can wait for me in the car."

Red didn't like that idea at all, but there wasn't much he could say. He knew that because of the crutches he couldn't get around very well.

"All right," he said. "But you be careful. If that's Gar in that house, you don't want him to catch you."

Truer words were never spoken. I shut the door of the truck very quietly when I got out.

"You forget something?" Red asked before I'd taken five steps.

I knew immediately what he meant. I'd left the pistol on the seat. I went back to get it, and Red said, "You want to take this one?"

He held up the magnum, and I shook my head. I wasn't even sure I wanted to take the .38. I had a feeling that if Gar came after me, I was going to need more than a pistol. A rocket-propelled grenade launcher, maybe.

Thunder rumbled somewhere toward the north as I walked to where I could peer around the funny-looking hill. The clouds continued to thicken, making the middle of the day almost as dark as late afternoon. The wind was whipping dirt up off the road, and grit popped against my jeans. I could smell the rain, and I knew it couldn't be too far away now.

I saw no movement either in the house or the hangar, and then there was a flash of lightning, followed instantly by a crash of thunder almost directly overhead. When the noise died away, in the distance I could hear the rain rattling off the leaves of the trees.

I knew that if I waited for a few seconds the rain would reach me, and while it wouldn't make me invisible it would give me a much better chance to get to the hangar without being seen by whoever was in the house. If there was really anyone in there at all.

I jammed the .38 in the waistband of my jeans and pulled my sweatshirt over it. I looked back at the truck. Red was watching me through the windshield. I gave him a thumbs-up, and then the cold rain sluiced over me.

18

BY THE TIME I'd taken five steps, my sweatshirt and jeans had absorbed so much water that they felt as if they weighed twenty pounds.

I didn't mind. The rain was shielding me, and with the darkness that had come along with it there wasn't much chance that anyone glancing out a window of the little house would see anything other than a moving shadow.

I had to be careful not to fall. The grass was thin, and the rain was making the ground slick and treacherous. Water ran down my hair and into my eyes.

When I reached the metal building, I checked the sliding door. I hadn't seen a lock, but the door had been quite a distance from the truck.

There was no lock, just a hasp pushed over an iron loop. I pulled the hasp back and pushed the door. It moved a couple of inches along its track with a shrill, squealing noise. The rain was beating so hard on the metal roof that no one was going to hear the squeal more than a few feet away, however, so I pushed the door open wide enough to allow me to slip inside the building.

It was dark inside, and the darkness smelled of dirt and spiderwebs. I wiped water out of my eyes and listened to the rain drumming on the metal roof.

The plane was there, all right. Or *a* plane was there, white monoplane that looked like the crop duster that ha strafed us. It was more than likely the same one.

As I stood there looking at the plane, I heard the squea of the door above the static of the rain on the roof. Instead oi turning to see who was coming in, I ducked down and ran toward a pile of boxes in a shadowy corner.

There was a series of *phhhhhttttt*s behind me as I ran, and the boxes twitched as if they were alive.

I made a sharp left turn, hit the dirt, and slid ten feet, the pistol grinding into my belly. Bullets flew over my head and spanged through the metal walls.

I rolled over and clawed at my soaking sweatshirt, try-ing to get to the .38. When I got it out of my waistband, I fired once into the air just to let whoever was shooting at me know I had a gun, too. My eyes had adjusted somewhat to the lack of light, and I looked around to see what I could see.

I'd managed to get the biplane between me and the shooter, so I could see only his legs in the dimness. They were as thick as tree stumps, and I knew it must be Gar. I snapped off a shot at his combat boots, but the bullet missed him and ricocheted off the floor and into the wall.

I didn't shoot again. The revolver didn't hold quite as many rounds as whatever Gar was using, and I hadn't brought any spare cartridges. They were all in the truck where they would do me no good at all, and I couldn't afford to waste any more.

I rolled toward the wall as quietly as I could, hoping there might be some way out of the building other than the door, maybe a window, although I hadn't seen one.

Gar still hadn't said a word, not that I'd expected him to. He didn't seem fond of conversation even in social situations more relaxed than this one.

I looked for his feet again. They were moving toward the tail of the plane. He was going to get me for sure, though I might have time for one shot.

I sat up slowly, my back pressed against the cold metal of the wall, and steadied the .38 with both hands. As big as he was, even if I hit him, I probably wouldn't bring him down, not unless I could hit him in the knee or the shin. Even then, he might be able to fire off a whole clip while he was falling. A head shot would be better, but in the dim light, with a gun I'd fired only twice before, a head shot didn't seem practical.

I wouldn't have given a lot at that moment for my chances of getting out of the hangar alive, but I tried not to dwell on that thought. It wouldn't improve my aim.

I had the pistol pointed at about where I figured Gar's legs would be when he came around the tail of the plane. One chance was all I was going to get. Water was running down my hair and forehead, into my face. Or maybe it was sweat. I wiped it away and gripped the pistol again. My finger tightened on the trigger.

Before I could shoot, a booming noise echoed off all four walls and made me jump straight up off the ground. It was as if the thunder from outside had come into the building with me. Something that seemed about the size of a cannonball tore a hole through the metal wall at one end of the building.

"All right, Gar," Red yelled. "Put down that rifle and turn around."

I didn't know Gar intimately, but he didn't seem like the

type to be afraid of a little thing like a .357 magnum. I had to do something to help Red out, so I stood up and said, "Give it up, Gar. We've got you surrounded."

The Durango Kid would have been proud of me.

Gar probably didn't know who the Durango Kid was. And if he'd known, he wouldn't have cared. Most likely, he would have shot him.

Red knew that, and he didn't give Gar a chance to shoot. He fired the magnum again.

I suspect that he was thinking about Paul and that he was trying to kill Gar, but it didn't work out that way. The bullet hit Gar's automatic rifle and ripped it out of his hands.

I moved with the shot and got around the plane in time to see what happened next. Gar ran straight at Red, who was balancing himself on his crutches and firing the magnum with both hands.

If Gar had been charging me, I would have been nervous, and Red was no better than me. He fired three shots, all of which missed, and then Gar slammed into him like a line-backer trying to tackle Emmitt Smith.

Red was no Emmitt. He flew backward at least six feet, and hit the ground hard, dropping the pistol.

Gar pounced on the gun and picked it up. Then he whirled to face me.

"It's empty, Gar," I said. "But mine's not."

He still didn't say a word. Instead, with that incredible quickness of his, he threw the pistol at me, a trick I'd seen tried in dozens of old movies.

It never worked in the movies, but it worked for Gar. He had an arm like Nolan Ryan. I tried to duck out of the way, but the pistol butt hit me on the temple. The pain shot from my head to my spine and then traveled all the way down to my toes. I looked for Gar, but I couldn't see him. I couldn't see anything at all.

THE NEXT THING I heard was the sound of the rain on the metal roof and above that the sound of the plane's engine revving. The vibrations nearly shook my skull apart.

I looked up at the plane. Gar was in the cockpit, and he didn't look the least bit airsick. I pushed myself to my knees and picked up my pistol as the plane began to roll out the open door.

I was determined not to let Gar escape, so I got to my feet and staggered after him. Red lay on the dirt, either unconscious or dead. I didn't have time to check.

I got myself into a kind of shambling run, with each step sending shock waves of pain through my head. I put my hand on my damp hair and pressed down to keep the top of my skull where it belonged.

I caught up with the plane just as it passed through the door. The rain had slowed considerably, and the wind had died down. Gar gunned the plane's engine and pulled away from me, out onto the runway.

I didn't know much about flying, but I'd always heard that a plane was supposed to take off with its nose pointed into the wind. If I was right, Gar had to taxi to the end of the open area, turn around, and come back in my direction. I stumbled along behind him, my feet slipping in the mud, and tried to remember how many shots I'd fired.

Two? Three? I had no idea.

Gar reached the end of the runway and turned the plane slowly. Then he headed back toward me, gradually picking up speed. I thought I could see him grinning in the cockpit, but I knew I was just imagining it.

I stopped running and brought up the pistol, gripping it with both hands. I was none too steady, and it shook more than a little. There was no help for that, however, and I squeezed off a shot.

Nothing happened, and I fired again and then again. After that the hammer clicked on an empty cylinder, and that was all the shooting I could do. I either had to get out of the way or get chopped in two by the propeller.

I got out of the way.

I dived to the slick ground and slid forward, and then I had another bad idea. I flipped over on my back. When the plane passed over me, I reached up to grab one of the struts that braced the left wheel.

I'm not sure what I planned to do. Maybe I was thinking about some old movie I'd seen, where the hero climbed aboard the plane and gracefully walked along the wing, then grabbed the villain's silk flying scarf, yanked him out of the cockpit, and tossed him to the earth before taking over the plane and steering it down for a perfect three-point landing.

While there isn't much doubt that Gar was a first-class villain, I wasn't exactly graceful, and I wasn't much of a hero. So things didn't work the way they did in old movies.

My arms were almost jerked from their sockets, and suddenly I was bouncing over the ground a lot faster than I would have thought possible. Every time my back hit, I yelled. I don't think Gar could hear me. I don't think he would have cared if he'd heard.

He must have known I was there, though. He would have felt the drag, and he would have known that he couldn't get the altitude he needed as quickly as he needed it.

He had to give it a try, though, and he almost made it. I found myself dangling in the air, only my toes dragging, and we were rushing straight at a huge mound of dirt that marked the end of the runway.

He probably thought he could gain enough altitude to get over the mound or, failing that, get high enough so that I would be mashed against the mound like a bug against a windshield.

I didn't much like that idea of being flattened, but I wasn't about to let go and let Gar get away. I pumped my arms, swung my legs, and bounced up and down as hard as I could.

The unexpected pitching and swaying pulled the left wing down, suddenly and dangerously. Gar tried to correct, but it was too late. He wasn't going to get airborne.

Now I was willing to let go. I dropped to the ground just before the plane crashed into the hillock.

The fall almost jarred my head off my neck, and my bad knee gave way beneath me. I rolled over two or three times before I came to a stop. I heard the crash but didn't see it. I lay like a rock for several seconds before I was able to stand and look around.

The plane had hit hard enough to cause severe damage to the front end, but it hadn't hit hard enough to finish the job: Gar wasn't dead. He didn't even seem to be hurt badly as he pulled himself out of the cockpit.

He was, however, really pissed off, and he headed straight for me. He slipped twice, falling almost to his knees before he caught himself. The falls didn't cheer him up any. They just made him angrier.

There was a thin string of smoke rising from the plane's engine, and I hoped it might explode into one of those spectacular fireballs you see in the movies sometimes, sending debris flying everywhere, maybe even sending a chunk of it right into the head of the survivor.

There was no explosion, of course. Instead there was a noise that sounded like fifty pounds of bacon frying, but that was all, and Gar kept right on coming.

It's not exactly manly to admit it, but I think I would have run from him if I could have. The trouble was that I couldn't.

I wasn't even sure I could walk. So I just stood there, waiting for Gar.

The rain had almost completely stopped, and when Gar got a little closer, I could see that he wasn't in quite as good shape as I'd first thought.

He'd lost his cap, and his little ponytail had come loose. His hair was wet and hanging around his face, his left eye was half closed, and there was a long scratch down his cheek. Blood oozed from the scratch. It didn't improve his looks any.

I thought he might say something, curse me, scream at me, call me a name, but of course he didn't. When he got close enough, he just swung at me with a long, impossibly quick right arm and knocked the crap out of me.

I'd just *thought* my head hurt before. Now it *really* hurt, and I was pretty sure that he'd dislocated my jaw.

After a second or two I realized that I was sitting down. I didn't even remember falling. Gar came over and reached for me. He grabbed my sweatshirt, squeezing about a quart of water out of it as he dragged me to my feet. He held me at arm's length as he prepared to club me again with his big fist.

I didn't think I could stand another one of those blows. I grabbed the arm that held me, bent down, and sank my teeth into the soft webbing between his thumb and forefinger.

Gar screamed. It was nice to know that he could make a sound if given the right incentive. The scream encouraged me, and I didn't let go. I just clamped down harder.

Truman Smith, pit bull.

Gar's face turned red and swelled with rage. He took hold of my hair and yanked my head backward while he jerked his hand up and away from me.

I kept my teeth clenched shut, but if his aim was to tear himself loose, it worked. He did lose a pound of flesh in the process, though. My mouth filled with skin and blood and slick gristle.

I was trying to spit the foul mess out when he hit me again, not hard because he slipped as he swung and almost missed me. It was worse than being hit hard, though, because his fist glanced off my chin and made me swallow involuntarily. Part of his thumb webbing went right down my throat.

Truman Smith, cannibal.

I staggered back, gagged, and tried not to think about what I'd swallowed. I had to concentrate on staying alive. I couldn't run, but maybe I could stop Gar by going for his knee. I didn't have the gun, so I couldn't shoot the knee, but if I got lucky, I could kick it.

I kept backing up, and Gar kept coming after me. Blood was streaming from his hand, though he didn't seem to notice. It had started to rain hard again, and the blood was washing right off and disappearing on the ground. Gar kept his eyes fixed on my face as if visualizing how it would look after he crushed my nose and broke all my teeth.

I let him get as close as I dared, and when he planted his right knee to take another step, I aimed a swift kick at the kneecap.

Actually, "swift" is a slight exaggeration, maybe even a wild exaggeration, but I did the best I could do at the time, and it's hard to say who was more surprised when the kick connected, me or Gar.

He yelped and collapsed on both knees, so I stepped forward and hit him with a solid right/left combination before he could get back up. I might as well have been hitting a fence post for all the good I did.

Gar glared at me and popped to his feet. I didn't think he'd let me get away with kicking him again, so I decided to try another punch or two before he gathered his wits together.

I'd forgotten one thing. Gar didn't live by his wits. He lived by speed and instinct and reaction time, and his reaction time was something to behold. He hit me again, and this time I didn't even see it coming, probably with good reason. It landed so hard that it must have come by way of Antarctica.

I felt my brain come loose behind my eyes and bounce around in my head like a Nerf ball in a coffee can.

He hit me one more time, and I went down and out.

Truman Smith, dead man.

19

I WASN'T DEAD, however. If I were dead, I would have been feeling much better than I was. And if I were dead, there wouldn't be someone poking me in the left side with a muddy crutch.

I opened my eyes and looked up.

"You gonna be all right?" Red asked.

"I don't think so," I said, closing my eyes again.

I didn't try to sit up. I just lay there and let the rain fall on me. It wasn't falling very hard. I let a little of it run into my mouth to wash out the lingering taste of Gar's blood.

Red poked me with the crutch. "You're gonna catch pneumonia if you don't get some dry clothes on."

I didn't move. I didn't open my eyes, either. "What about Gar?"

"He's gone. Got in his truck and took off."

"Did you see him go?"

"Yeah. I was comin' out of the hangar."

"How'd he look?"

"A hell of a lot better than you do."

I wasn't surprised. I must have looked like a stunt double on the set of *Son of the Slime Monster*—a stunt double whose big gag had just gone very wrong.

"We found the airplane, though, didn't we?" I said.

"Yeah. And we kept Gar from gettin' it away from here and hidin' it someplace else." Red looked over at the wrecked crop duster. "I don't think anybody'll be movin' it now."

I opened my eyes and tried to sit up. I did, and it didn't hurt quite as much as I'd thought it would, not any more than getting run over by a buffalo stampede, so I tried to go farther and stand. I found I could do even that, though I was a little wobbly. I put a hand on Red's shoulder to steady myself.

"How did you get out here on those crutches?" I asked.

"It wasn't easy," Red said, looking down where the rubber tips were sunk half an inch into the mud. "You think the two of us can make it to the truck without fallin' down and breakin' our necks?"

I looked toward the mound where I'd parked the truck. It wasn't much more than a hundred yards. It looked like a hundred miles.

"We might as well give it a try," I said.

WE GOT TO the truck after what seemed like an eternity. My feet kept slipping, and Red's crutches sank into the mud so that he had to pull them out with a wet, sucking sound at every step.

It was dry inside the cab when we finally got there, but our clothes were drenched. I started the engine and turned on the heater.

"You got any money with you?" Red asked.

"In my billfold. It's probably wet."

"It'll do. We gotta find us a Wal-Mart and buy some clothes. Maybe a towel, too."

"I have a towel behind the seat," I said.

I got out, and Red leaned forward. I pulled the seat back over and got out the towel. It was dusty and had a few oil stains on it, but it would do. I got back in the cab and dried my face and hair, cleaning off most of the mud. There wasn't much I could do about my clothes. When I was finished, I handed the towel to Red.

"I have to do something else before we leave," I said.

"What?"

"Find our pistols."

"Yeah," Red said, rubbing his thinning hair with the towel. "You better do that. Prob'ly got our fingerprints all over 'em. Wouldn't do to leave 'em lyin' around. Somebody might get the idea that we were dangerous."

I had to laugh at that. The two of us were about as dangerous as a pair of bunny rabbits.

It didn't take long to locate the pistols. I seemed to be loosening up a little, and I wasn't quite as sore as I had been. Moving around helped. I wished I had a couple of ibuprofen. Or more than a couple. I promised myself that I'd buy a bottle when I got the dry clothes.

"Guns'll need a good cleanin'," Red said when I got back in the cab and laid them on the seat. "I'll have to do that this evenin'." He paused. "What are we gonna do when we get back?"

"Talk to Peavy," I said.

I FELT A lot better wearing a clean sweatshirt and jeans. The woman at the check-out counter at Wal-Mart hadn't even blinked at my muddy clothes. Maybe she saw guys dressed that way all the time.

The ibuprofen improved my outlook, too. I didn't even mind when Red complained that the pants and shirt I'd bought for him didn't fit right. He had to admit that at least they were dry and clean. He was still concerned about me, though.

"You sure you don't need to go by the emergency room?" he asked.

"I'll be all right," I said.

I hoped I was telling the truth. The ibuprofen was working, but my head still felt as if someone had blown up a balloon inside it, my lips were puffy, and my jaw still felt funny. I wasn't sure my teeth were meeting in the right place when I closed my mouth.

On the other hand, I could see and I could drive. I could hold my head up and I could breathe. I didn't see any reason to complain, not considering what Gar could have done to me if he'd had a little more time.

Maybe Gar and I could meet again someday. I hoped that if we did, I was much better armed. I'd been right about him from the first. A .38 wasn't big enough. Maybe a rocket-propelled grenade launcher wouldn't be enough. I began thinking along the lines of a Sidewinder missile.

"You think Peavy'll do anything about that airplane?" Red asked, breaking into my thoughts.

"He'll have to," I said. "But it doesn't prove anything by itself. You and I are convinced that Gar used it to strafe us yesterday, but the fact that the plane's on Evans's property isn't evidence of that. We can't even prove that Evans knew it was there."

"That son of a bitch killed my boy."

I didn't know whether he meant Gar or Evans. Right then it didn't seem to make much difference.

"Evans sent Gar up here to move that plane," Red went on. "He must've known we were comin' to look."

I'd wondered about that. I didn't recall telling anyone where we were going. Red claimed that he hadn't, either.

"But there were folks at Paul's house who might have heard me say something," he added.

"They weren't Evans's friends," I pointed out.

"You can't ever tell about that. Lots of folks listen to that radio show, and they all like Ralph."

"We'll let Peavy figure it out," I said.

Red said, "Hah."

I didn't have anything to add to that.

IT WAS NEARLY four o'clock when we got back to Picketville. I took Red by Anne's before going to the jail. There were still several cars parked in front of the house. I saw Martin York's Ford and Lance's black Acura parked side by side, felt a stab of jealousy, and then immediately felt guilty. Paul Lindeman had been dead only a few hours and already I was thinking about courting his widow.

"You gonna come in?" Red asked.

"No. I want to talk to Peavy while I'm still able to."

"You don't look too good, sure enough. You better go take a long nap when you get finished with him."

He got out of the truck and went slowly toward the door on his crutches. I was sorry for him, and I was sorry for Anne. I was even a little sorry for myself because I didn't know what the hell was going on. I'd come to town to find out who'd killed a prairie chicken, and now Paul Lindeman had been murdered and I'd been shot at from a biplane and been beaten half to death by the Amazing Colossal Man.

Things weren't going exactly as I'd planned.

I watched Red all the way to the porch, and when the door swung open, I turned the truck in the direction of the courthouse, which was several blocks off the highway, not far from the doctor's office where I'd taken Red.

The jail and sheriff's offices were in opposite wings of the courthouse building, a big gray concrete affair that depressed rather than inspired. It looked like something from the thirties, maybe a WPA project.

I walked into the sheriff's offices, and the receptionist looked at me as if I were a jail trusty who had wandered into the wrong wing.

"I'd like to talk to Sheriff Peavy," I told her. "My name's Truman Smith."

She never took her eyes off me as she picked up the phone and buzzed him.

Peavy walked out of his office to meet me. "You look like you came out on the losing end of a wrestling match with a rhino, Smith. What happened?"

"Let's go in your office," I said. "Then I'll tell you all about it."

"I bet it'll be mighty interesting, too," he said. "Hold my calls, Jane."

"Yes, Sheriff," the receptionist said, still looking at me as if she thought I might go for her throat at any moment.

When we were in Peavy's office, he closed the door behind us and said, "Have a seat, Smith, and tell me what's going on. Been sticking your nose where it doesn't belong?"

He walked around his desk and sat in a big, comfortable-looking chair, and I took the smaller, less appealing one opposite him. It wasn't even real leather.

"I guess you could say I stuck my nose where it doesn't belong," I said. "I was trespassing, which amounts to about the same thing."

I went on to tell him the whole story, slightly abridged to leave out the gunplay and the part about Red picking the lock on the gate. Even the cleaned-up version didn't make Peavy very happy.

"You know, Smith," he said when I was finished, "I'm the sheriff of this county. I'm the one with a badge. Not you. Not

Red Lindeman. I can sort of understand why Red would do something stupid like that. After all, it's his boy that was killed. But not you. You're supposed to know something about the law, and here you go, running off like some kind of vigilante. If you'd gotten killed, it would have served you right."

"Thanks," I said. "I appreciate your sympathy."

"That's real funny. But let me tell you something. If you go messing around again like that, I'm going to arrest you and see how long I can keep you locked up before some bleeding-heart lawyer finds out about you and busts you out."

I knew that he didn't really mean it. If he'd meant it, he wouldn't have given me a warning. So I shouldn't have said anything at all. But I did.

"Like you did the man who hanged himself?"

Peavy stood up, his hands balled into fists at his sides. "Who told you about that?"

"Why? Is it supposed to be a secret?"

His hands slowly relaxed. "No, it's not supposed to be a secret, but it's something else that's none of your damn business. And that's all I have to say about it."

He sat back down and stared at me. Maybe he thought he could scare me, but a man who'd been mixing it up with Gar Thornton wasn't likely to be scared of a mere county sheriff, even one who was threatening to arrest him.

"What about Gar?" I asked. "Are you going to look for him?"

"Sure I am. I'll look for him as soon as I have Denbow check out that airplane and make sure your story's true. Why? Do you think I don't know how to do my job?"

"I've been told that you and Ralph Evans are pretty good friends."

That brought him to his feet again. He put his palms flat on the desk and leaned toward me.

"Denbow was right about you, Smith," he said. "You're

a wiseass. And what's worse, you're wrong about everything. You don't even have a clue. I think you'd better get out of here now. Otherwise I might do something that we'll both be sorry for."

I stood up slowly, which was the only way I *could* stand up, and smiled at him.

"If I'm so wrong about everything," I said, "why don't you clue me in?"

"Because it's none of your business. You're in over your head, Smith. Now get out of here. And go back to Galveston before you get hurt."

"Too late for that," I said, and then I got out of there.

20

W H AT I N E E D E D was a long, hot shower and a nap. But those things would have to wait. I was getting really curious about the man who'd hanged himself at the jail, so I drove out to the radio station to see if Tony Lopez was still there.

As I drove I turned on the radio and tuned in KLWG. The news was on, and the newscaster closed the program by saying, "This is Tony Lopez for KLWG news. For the news and weather together, tune in KLWG at the top of every hour. We'll be there for you."

I'd missed the news, but at least I knew that Lopez was at the station. That was all I cared about.

It was a little early for the Ralph Evans crowd, and the parking lot was nearly empty. I went in and located the broadcasting booth. There were two men inside, one of them the engineer and one of them probably Lopez. One was wearing jeans and a T-shirt with a picture of Tweety Bird on it. The engineer, I thought. The other was wearing Dockers and a sports shirt. I figured that had to be Lopez. I tapped on the glass, and when he looked around, I motioned for him to come outside.

He was young and handsome, probably not more than twenty-five, shorter than I was, with slick, black hair, black eyes, and a smooth complexion. He had a deep voice that sounded even deeper in person than it had on the radio.

"What can I do for you?" he asked.

I asked if he was Lopez, and when he said that he was, I told him my name and what I was doing there. He suggested that we go to his office to talk. It was next door to Paul's office and only a little smaller.

"Paul told me about you," he said when we were inside. "But I guess you're not really interested in prairie chickens now. Are you going to be investigating his murder?"

I was already investigating it, but not officially, and there wasn't likely to be any official sanction of anything I did, not as long as Peavy was sheriff. He didn't seem to like me much.

However, considering the story that Lopez was working on, I thought he might not be the sheriff's best friend, either. So I told him the truth.

"I'm looking into the murder, all right, but I'm not working with the sheriff. And the whole thing's got me wondering about something else, something that you might be able to help me with."

"I liked Paul a lot," Lopez said. "He gave me this job, and he taught me nearly everything I know about radio. I'll do whatever I can."

"I don't want you to do anything," I said. "I just need some information."

"What about?"

"About the man who hanged himself in the jail."

Suddenly Lopez wasn't quite so eager to help. He dropped his eyes to his desk.

"I don't know if I should talk to you about that," he said.

"Why not?"

"I'm not sure Paul would have wanted me to."

"You said you wanted to help me, and Paul's dead. What he might have wanted doesn't matter now."

Lopez's head jerked up. "How can you say that?"

I didn't say anything. I just let him think about it. Finally he said, "OK. Maybe you're right. You probably are, because I think the hanged man does have something to do with Paul's murder."

"Tell me about it."

He leaned back in his chair. "All right. I don't know who the man was, but Paul did. I'm not sure how. Paul wouldn't tell me just exactly what was going on, but he was convinced that the hanging wasn't suicide. The sheriff did an investigation that cleared his office of any blame, but Paul wasn't satisfied with that."

"Why?" I asked. "He must have had a reason."

Lopez nodded. "I'm sure he did, but he never came right out and told me. I think I know, though. I guess you want to hear about it."

I guessed I wanted to hear about it, too.

"Tell me," I said.

"I think the man had been doing something for Paul, some kind of undercover work. Maybe an investigation into the sheriff's office. I asked Paul, but he wouldn't say. He'd just say it was private and that he didn't want to talk about it."

"Was that all there was to it?"

"Yes. Except for the way the man died."

"He hanged himself. What's suspicious about that?"

"Look," Lopez said, "he was drunk when he was arrested, right?"

"That's what I was told."

"OK. And there's no question about that part of it. The night he got arrested, he'd been out at the Longhorn Club. You know where that is?"

Red and I had driven past it on our way to Evans's land.

It was a long, low building just off the highway, with a gravel parking lot and a peeling paint job. The sign out front had a crude drawing of a longhorn's head on it.

"I've seen the place," I said.

"Well, he'd had plenty to drink there according to the bartender, and he got in a little discussion with a couple of guys who didn't like the way he was looking at their dates. The discussion got ugly, and a fight started. That's what led to the arrest."

I wasn't sure where this was going. "So the guy's drunk and in jail. He hangs himself out of humiliation or because he just doesn't know what he's doing. Is that it?"

"That's probably what the sheriff would like everyone to believe. But I don't. Believe it, I mean. And neither would anyone else who'd ever been in that jail cell. Have you ever seen it?"

"I haven't had the pleasure."

"The bars are nearly seven feet off the floor, probably to prevent the possibility of anybody hanging himself, especially somebody about five six or seven, which is what this guy was. He couldn't reach the bars to tie anything to them. And the cot's bolted to the floor five feet away from the window. There's no way anyone could stand on the cot and tie anything to those bars."

I was beginning to get the picture. "So he had a little help."

Lopez frowned. "Or a lot of help. He must have. And he had a visitor."

Now here was some news worth knowing. "Who?"

"But the visitor swore that the man was alive when he left the cell."

"So would I if I'd hanged him. Who was the visitor?"

"He's a big guy. He could have hung that little guy with no trouble at all."

Tony really knew how to drag out a story. "OK, OK. Tell me who it was."

I thought I'd already figured it out, so I wasn't at all surprised when he said, "Gar Thornton."

THERE WAS MORE to the story, of course. There's always more. Gar had been one of the men at the Longhorn Club, and he'd been involved in both the "discussion" and the fight.

"Gar can talk?" I said.

"When he wants to." Lopez grinned. "He usually doesn't want to. Hell, he doesn't *have* to."

I knew what he meant. "If he got into an argument with Gar, the guy must have really been drunk."

"They did a blood test. Alcohol level was about twice the legal limit."

"You wouldn't think that would have affected his judgment enough to make him want to fight Gar."

"That's what Paul thought. He talked to the bartender, Roy Nobles, and Roy said it looked to him like Gar and his buddy picked the fight."

"Wait a minute. His buddy. That wouldn't be Bert Ware by any chance, would it?"

"No. It was some guy named Steve Stilwell, looks a little like Sam Elliott on a bad-hair day. Anyway, Gar and Bert don't hang out together. Except when they're doing bodyguard duty with Ralph."

"Do you think Paul could have had this man looking into something to do with Evans?"

"That could be. He wouldn't say. I think he would have told me sooner or later, but he just wasn't ready. He wanted to see what I could turn up first."

"What else have you found out?"

"Nothing, really. I just found out about Gar being the visitor a few days ago. I finally found somebody at the jail who'd talk to me about it. Gar came in and said that he wanted to apologize to the guy, that he was sorry he'd been arrested. So he got in to see him."

"And the jailer didn't notice anything funny when Gar left? Like a guy hanging from the bars?"

"He says he didn't. He may even be telling the truth. It was late at night, and he was probably sleepy. He might never even have looked into the cell, or Gar could have blocked his view. Gar's a pretty big guy."

I could vouch for that. "What did Paul say when you told him about Gar's visit?"

"He got really excited. He told me he had some calls to make and that he'd let me know more when he'd found out a few things. He never got around to it, though."

"What about the men who came to town later, the ones who seemed interested in the hanging?"

"I don't know about them. I mean, I know about them, but I don't know who they were or where they came from. They didn't give much away. The sheriff knows, I'll bet, since they spent a lot of time talking to him. But if he knows anything, he's not telling."

No surprise there. I didn't blame him. In a case like this, you needed to keep things as quiet as possible.

There was one other thing I wanted to know. I said, "What was the guy's name?"

"The one who hanged himself? It was Lloyd. Lloyd Abbott."

"Damn," I said.

"What?" Lopez asked.

"Lloyd Abbott. I know him, sort of. He's a private eye."

I'd met Abbott only once, but I remembered him. Short, loud, and with a reputation for hitting the bottle. And with exactly the right name to make him the kind of investigator

Paul Lindeman would hire if Paul had wanted a professional to look into irregularities in the sheriff's office. Abbott would have been one of the first private investigators listed in the Houston Yellow Pages. I wondered if he had a partner, and I knew I'd have to find out.

Lopez stood up. His chair squeaked, sounding a lot like the door at Evans's hangar. I winced.

"You don't look so good," Evans said. "Can I get you something to drink? We have a soda machine."

"Does it have Big Red?"

"Yeah. Nobody ever drinks it, though."

"I will, but I can get it myself." I stood up to prove how tough I was. "Show me the way."

We went out of the office and down the hall to the green-room. There was a machine in an alcove nearby, and I fished quarters out of my pocket and fed them into the coin slot.

"What about Abbott?" Lopez asked. "What do you think he was doing here?"

The Big Red clanked into the little tray near the bottom of the soda machine. I managed to get hold of the can and wiggle it out. Then I popped it open and took a swallow. It was better than ibuprofen.

"I'll see what I can find out about Abbott," I said after two more swallows. "I don't have any idea what he was doing here, but you could have been right about Paul being suspicious of Peavy's office. There's some kind of cover-up going on. I'm sure of that."

Lopez's news instincts came to the fore. "You'll let me know what you find out, won't you?"

"Sure," I said, but I didn't mean it. I was going to find out for Red and Paul and Anne, not to give anyone a big story.

I finished the Big Red and thanked Lopez for his help. Then, since I hadn't eaten all day, I went to The Toole Shed. It was time to try the famous jalapeño burger.

21

THE JALAPEÑO BURGER was even hotter than I'd imagined it would be, the bun stuffed with meat, onions, and fresh, bright-green peppers. But I survived it, thanks to several large glasses of ice water and an order of French fries. After I finished eating, I drove back out to the radio station. I might have needed some rest, but I didn't think I could sleep without having talked to Ralph Evans.

The station lobby was filled with pretty much the same group of men as before, but this time the conversation seemed to be mostly about Internet addresses for the home pages of groups like the NRA and the 2nd Amendment Foundation. From what I could overhear, it was clear that most of them were not just passive listeners to a radio show but were networking with like-minded souls all over the country and probably the world.

I didn't bother to say "Heighdy"; I just went on to the greenroom, and when I got there, I didn't knock.

Bert Ware grabbed my shoulder as soon as I stepped through the door, but I shook him off and walked over to where Evans was sitting, cleaning his fingernails with a pocketknife.

"Where's Gar Thornton?" I asked. "Does he have the night off?"

Bert grabbed for me again, and I turned to face him, knocking his arm away. He cocked a fist, and I set myself, hoping that he'd follow through. It would feel good to take on someone my own size. But Evans stopped him before he could swing.

"Never mind, Bert," he said. "Mr. Smith isn't bothering me, and he won't be here long."

Bert sneered and tried to look threatening, but he wasn't as good at it as Gar. And Gar didn't even have to try.

"Well?" I said. "Where's Gar?"

Evans folded the knife blade into the handle and put the knife in his pants' pocket. Then he inspected his fingernails for a second or two before looking up at me.

"To tell you the truth," he said, "I don't know where Gar is. And I don't really care."

"Why not? He works for you, doesn't he?"

"He used to," Evans admitted. "But I don't consider him my employee anymore. He had specific duties, and they didn't include stealing airplanes. I'm mighty disappointed in Gar. He told me that he got airsick on the second floor of a two-story building."

Obviously Peavy or Denbow had talked to Evans earlier, and Evans had already taken steps to distance himself from Gar.

"I'm a little disappointed in Gar, myself," I said. "Are you still going to tell me that he was having a hamburger with you when I got shot at?"

Evans shrugged. "I said it. I'll stick by it."

"You can stick by it if you want to," I said, "but considering that he tried to kill me, you won't be hurt if I don't buy it. And since you seem to know all about it, what I'd like to know is what that plane was doing on your property."

Evans smiled complacently, as if he didn't have a worry in the world.

"That's another reason I'm disappointed in the boy," he said. "I never thought he'd get me involved in something like shooting at honest citizens from an airplane, much less that he'd hide the plane on my own land in that old barn. But then it's awful hard to get good help these days. Except for Bert there. I can trust him. Can't I, Bert?"

I looked around. Bert was grinning and showing his teeth, which were better than Gar's, but not so much better that I enjoyed looking at them. I turned back to Evans.

"I think you're lying," I said. "I think Gar stole that plane for you, and I think you know where he is right now."

Evans stopped smiling and his face turned ugly. "That's a mighty dangerous accusation to make, Mr. Smith. It might even be called slanderous."

I didn't care about slander at that point, and as long as I was making dangerous accusations, I figured that I might as well make another one.

"Why did you have Gar kill Lloyd Abbott?" I asked.

"Who?"

"Lloyd Abbott, the man Gar hanged in his jail cell."

"I believe you're really trying to go too far, Mr. Smith. I heard about Gar's little set-to with that drunk out at the Long-horn Club, but Gar didn't have anything to do with hanging the man. The sheriff investigated that whole incident and found out that the man had killed himself. A clear-cut case of suicide. That was the ruling I heard. I think all the medical evidence pointed in that direction."

For a man who was willing to talk about all kinds of conspiracies on his radio show, Evans seemed exceptionally eager to accept that in Abbott's case there was absolutely no evidence of a cover-up.

And there was another problem. He was so calm, so reasonable, so sure that he was right, that I was almost beginning to believe him.

"I haven't heard about any medical evidence," I said. "Why don't you tell me about it."

Evans shrugged. "You'd have to talk to the sheriff about that. I don't know much about forensics. I'm just a radio talk-show host."

I'd nearly forgotten that I was dealing with a talk-show host, a man whose very job and career depended on how convincing he could sound. And he was good at his job. I shook off his arguments.

"I'm going to find Gar," I told him. "And when I do, I'm going to get the truth out of him."

"I hope you do," Evans said. "That's all any of us really want. Just the truth."

I turned to leave the room. Bert was still grinning and showing his teeth. I resisted the urge to try shoving them down his throat.

"So long, Smith," he said when I walked past him. "Be seein' you."

"Not if I see you first," I said.

Never let it be said that I'm ever at a loss for a snappy comeback.

I WAS SO tired that I was about to collapse, but I drove back into town to use the pay phone. When Dino answered, I told him I wanted him to find out a few things about a couple more people.

"Hey, what about your cat? You don't want to hear about him?"

"Tell me," I said.

"He's fine. Likes me more every time he sees me. He's always right there waiting for me. I think he knows the sound of my car."

He probably did. Cats have a finely developed sense about sounds associated with food.

"You're doing a great job," I said. "Now about those people I need to know about. Their names are Lloyd Abbott and Gar Thornton. Abbott was a PI in Houston, but he's dead now. Hanged himself in the jail here, or so everyone keeps telling me. Thornton is a bodyguard by profession, or he was until earlier today. As of then, he's a fugitive from justice. I want to know about what he used to be."

"You sound like you don't like him," Dino said.

"I don't."

"Why not?"

"It's a long story."

"Yeah. Well, I'll see what I can dig up. Give me a call in the morning."

"I'll give you a call later tonight," I said.

"I go to bed early these days."

"I'll try not to wake you."

"You're really pushing this, Tru. What's going on up there?"

"I told you. It's a long story."

"I want to hear about it, though."

"I'll tell you all about it when I get back to Galveston."

"You do that," he said.

I DROVE TO the Picketville Inn, showered, took some more ibuprofen, and lay down on the bed. I was asleep in under ten seconds, dreaming something about an airplane that was on a collision course with an active volcano. It was sort of a cross between *The High and the Mighty* and *Air-plane!*, with me playing both John Wayne and Leslie Nielsen. The telephone woke me as I was using my John Wayne voice to tell someone not to call me Shirley.

I fumbled around for the receiver and finally got it off the hook. It took another few seconds for me to get it to my ear and mouth.

"Hello?" I mumbled.

Red Lindeman said, "Is that you, Smith?"

I admitted that it was.

"I didn't wake you up, did I?"

I don't know how you answer that question. I make it a practice always to tell the truth.

"Yeah, you did."

"Damn. I'm sorry." He didn't sound sorry. "I just figured you hadn't heard about the visitation tonight."

"What visitation?" I asked.

"At the funeral home. The family's here from seven till nine for people to come by and pay their last respects to Paul."

I looked at the clock. It was seven-thirty. I'd been asleep for about half an hour.

"No one told me," I said.

"Yeah, that's what I thought. I knew you'd want to come by and say something to Anne."

I'd already said all I had to say, but I asked him for directions, and after he'd given them, I said, "I'll be there in fifteen minutes."

IT TOOK ME a little more than fifteen minutes, but not much. The short nap had made me feel somewhat better, and I wasn't as stiff as I would probably have been had I slept longer.

The funeral home was located next to a small private

cemetery shaded by large oak trees. The cemetery must have been there for quite a while.

I parked as close to the entrance of the funeral home as I could and walked inside. The funeral director welcomed me and asked me to sign the register. When I'd written my name, he guided me to the chapel, where organ music was being piped in over an unobtrusive sound system.

Several people were standing in the aisles, talking, while others were sitting in the pews down near the casket. I could see Red and Anne. Lance was sitting beside her. As far as I could tell, Martin York was nowhere around, and that was all right with me.

The casket was closed, and a spray of flowers lay across the top. Near the casket an easel held an oversized color photograph of Paul and Anne, taken at their wedding. They were standing in front of a church altar. Paul wore a tuxedo, and Anne wore a white gown. They were both young and hopeful and smiling. Anne wasn't smiling now, and Paul would never smile again.

I walked down to the front of the chapel and sat in the pew behind Red, who turned around to see who had come in.

"Good of you to come," he said, as if it had been my own idea. "I don't guess you've seen anything of York."

I said that I hadn't.

Anne turned and said, "I can't imagine where he could be. He said he was going to come by."

"He'll turn up," I said. I looked toward the casket. "That's a nice photograph."

"An old one," Anne said. She brushed a hand at her eyes. "It's the only good one I had. Paul didn't much like having his picture taken."

Lance put his arm around her shoulders. It was a gesture that practically implied possession, and I didn't like it. Red, however, didn't seem to mind, and I told myself that I shouldn't be jealous and stupid. Paul hadn't been dead for twenty-four hours. Lance wouldn't be making a move quite so soon.

"When is the funeral?" I asked.

"Tomorrow," Red said. "We don't believe in waiting long."

I didn't blame them.

"What about Gar Thornton?" Lance asked. "Red tells me you think he's the killer, and that Ralph Evans is involved."

I looked at Red. He looked right back.

"That's not exactly true," I said. "All I know is that Gar has some connection to the airplane that strafed us. How that ties in to Paul's death, I don't know. It might not tie in at all."

Lance was going to say more, but a man came into the chapel and walked quickly to where we were sitting.

Red said, "What's the problem, Jerry?"

Jerry, a big man with stiff, brush-cut hair and a broad face, said, "I thought you'd want to hear. They've just arrested Martin York for killing Paul."

22

THERE WERE TWO pillows on my bed at the Picketville Inn, and they couldn't have been more than an inch thick. I plumped them up as much as I could, propped them against the bed's headboard, and leaned back against them.

The visitation had broken up with the news of York's arrest. Red had gone home with Anne, and Lance and I had come back to the Inn, where Lance had his own room, the same one he stayed in whenever he visited the town. I was willing to bet that the pillows in his room were thicker than the ones I was leaning against.

I'd gotten a Big Red from the motel's soda machine, and I took a swallow of it, savoring its bubble-gum sweetness as I tried to make all the things that had happened in the past few days fit into some kind of coherent pattern.

It had all started with the prairie chicken, and I was no closer to finding out who had killed it than I'd been when I'd arrived in Picketville. But the prairie chicken didn't seem to be important now, endangered species or not.

Human beings were the ones in trouble now.

It was hard to figure Martin York for a killer of either a man or a bird. The only evidence against him seemed to be that he'd been picked up by Deputy Denbow for doing forty-five miles an hour in a thirty-mile zone, and Denbow had spotted a shotgun in the back of his car.

It wasn't that there's anything particularly unusual in a Texan carrying around a shotgun that made Denbow order York out of the car. It was that York was one of the least likely Texans to be carrying one, especially within a day of Paul Lindeman having been killed with the same kind of weapon.

I'd driven by Peavy's office on the way back to the Inn and gotten the story from Peavy himself. The gun had been fired recently, and when confronted with it, York had reacted violently, shoving Denbow down, kicking him, and trying to escape in his car.

Denbow shot out one of the front tires, and York had swerved over the curb and plowed into a tree before he'd gotten to the next cross street. He was under arrest now, and sitting in the same cell that Lloyd Abbott had been in before his unfortunate death by hanging, which was either a suicide or a murder, depending on what you wanted to believe.

I hoped that he would survive to stand trial, if he had one. Quite a few people at the funeral home seemed ready to hang him on the spot. But maybe they just didn't like him.

I had to admit that he wasn't exactly the most likable person around town, from my point of view. He had been far more attentive to Anne than I thought was seemly, and he'd tried to show off when he shook my hand. But the fact that nobody liked him wasn't reason enough to convict him of murder.

Even Peavy had to agree with that, but when I mentioned it, he said, "Maybe not. But I think we've got the right man.

We're going to search his house, and I think we'll find some evidence that will get us a conviction."

He seemed awfully sure of that, and I wondered if he might be going to plant the evidence himself, or have Deputy Denbow plant it.

"What kind of evidence?" I asked.

"That's the department's business, Smith. You can go on back to Galveston now. We don't have any reason to hold you in town now, and we sure don't need your help doing our job."

"Speaking of doing your job, what did Denbow find up at Evans's place?"

"The plane was there, just like you said it was."

"So? Doesn't that implicate Evans?"

"He says he didn't know the plane was there. He didn't even know Gar could fly a plane."

"OK, if that's his angle, I guess you've got an all-points out on Gar. After all, he was trying to kill me and Red."

"Maybe he was just having a little fun. He might've taken the plane for a little joyride, seen you two, and cut loose with his rifle. Just to scare you."

"He scared me. He might have done more than that to Paul Lindeman."

"We'll ask him all about it when we catch up with him. But we've got the man who killed Lindeman already."

I didn't think so, but there was no way I was going to convince Peavy that he was wrong.

"Just one little tip before I go," I said.

"What's that?"

"Don't let Gar Thornton visit Martin York. I'd hate to see York end up hanging from the bars like your other prisoner."

"Denbow was sure right about you, Smith. Someday your mouth's going to write a check your ass can't cash."

"We'll see," I said.

Snappy replies are my stock-in-trade.

A S I T H O U G H T about Martin York now, the possibility of his guilt seemed even less likely than it had earlier. Oh, you could make a plausible argument that York was guilty of Paul's murder if you wanted to. You might even be able to argue that York had killed the prairie chicken.

Say he was in love with Anne, which was a pretty good likelihood. Killing the bird might serve to bring them together, in the search for the guilty party, as indeed it seemed to have done. But that was all it had done. Paul Lindeman was still in the way. The shotgun had worked on the bird. Why not try it out on the man?

It was plausible, all right, but that was all. It wasn't convincing, and I didn't believe a word of it. It left too much unexplained. The strafing and Gar's actions with the plane, for example. Where did they fit into things? Did York even know Gar? I'd asked Red about that before I'd left the funeral home, and he'd said that as far as he knew, York had no connection with Gar.

Of course, there was that shotgun in York's car. I wasn't sure how to explain that, but there were plenty of shotguns around, just as there were plenty of other candidates for Paul Lindeman's murder.

There was Sheriff Peavy, for one. Lindeman knew something about the hanging of Lloyd Abbott. I was sure of that, just as I was sure that Abbott hadn't committed suicide.

And Peavy knew something, too. Just what, I wasn't certain. But something. Could it be that he was protecting someone at the jail?

Denbow came to mind. How did he happen to stop York for speeding? I wouldn't think that the deputies regularly patrolled the streets of Picketville for speeders. Or maybe it wasn't Peavy who was protecting someone. Maybe it was Denbow.

Then there was Ralph Evans. I didn't think he'd done anything himself, but he could have had it done. That would be more his style.

Killing the prairie chicken might have been symbolically important to him, or he might have had it in for Lance because the station was going to drop his show. Since Lindeman was the moving force behind dropping the show, Evans wouldn't have regretted his death.

And of course there was a rumored connection between Peavy and Evans's Minute Men. Maybe there was something going on there that was worth investigating.

Or maybe Gar had been acting alone, out of his loyalty to Evans. I could believe that easily enough of Gar, and even of Bert, though I wasn't sure Bert had the brains to find his fanny with a flashlight.

I couldn't help thinking that there was something in all of this that I was overlooking, something so basic that I should have seen it immediately, sitting right out in the open like that letter in the Poe story.

But maybe not. I finished off the Big Red and set the can on the nightstand. I sat up and looked at the bedside clock. 9:47. Time to call Dino and see what, if anything, he had for me.

ON MY WAY to the pay phone, I tuned in Ralph Evans. He sounded as smooth as ever, and his topic for the moment was militia groups, specifically his own Minute Men.

"Now I know that there are racist groups out there," he said. "I'm not so naive that I don't know that there are groups full of people like that Mark Fuhrman who lied about using the 'n' word at the O. J. Simpson trial. And I guess it's even true that some groups are full of subversive types who want to overthrow the government of this great land of ours, the kind of scum who wreck trains and blow up buildings and kill innocent men, women, and children.

"But I'm here to tell you that the Picketville Minute Men aren't a bit like that. There's not a person I know who would ever be involved in any kind of violence or illegal act. Sure, we're worried about the way the power of big government keeps growing and growing, and we're worried about how they're trying to take all our rights away, but we're not going to kill anybody to put a stop to abuses like that. We're committed to working for changes through all the legitimate channels, and we don't want any kooks joining us.

"Now while you're pondering that, let's have a few words about some of our great sponsors. After that I'll be back to take some more of your calls."

Once again he sounded completely convincing, and he might have been talking directly to me. I wondered for a second if there were some way he could tell the exact second that I'd turned on my radio.

But of course he wasn't talking to me. He was reassuring his sponsors and his listeners, and maybe even Lance Garrison, saying that he was really a responsible citizen and that they didn't have to worry about his causing any trouble.

Now that Paul Lindeman was out of the way, maybe Evans really didn't even have to worry. He'd seemed awfully sure that Lance wouldn't cancel him.

I clicked off the radio and stopped at the pay phone. Candle flies swooped around the light that illuminated the handset, and I brushed them away from my face as I dropped in my quarter.

Dino answered on the first ring.

"What have you got for me?" I asked.

"You're sure in a hurry these days," he said. "No 'How's it going, Dino?' or social talk at all."

I sighed and said, "How's it going, Dino?"

"Pretty good. How's it with you?"

"Great. Now, what have you got?"

"I'm sorry I ever told you about Lance and his chicken," Dino said. "It's made you as impatient as a mainlander. I guess it was a bad idea."

"You got that right. But you did tell me, so give with the information."

"All right. Who you want first, Abbott or Thornton?"

"Why don't we do it alphabetically."

"Sure, why not? Lloyd Abbott was a PI in Houston, like you said. Got a little display ad in the Yellow Pages, nothing special, just about an eighth of a page."

"Is that all you did, look in the Yellow Pages?"

"Hey, you gotta start somewhere. You want to hear this or not?"

"Yeah. While you're at it, tell me where he was listed."

"Fourth investigator in the book, but the first ad."

That fit with what I'd thought. Paul picked Abbott, if he'd picked him, because he was the first prominent name in the Yellow Pages.

"OK. Tell me what the ad said."

"I thought you didn't want to hear this," Dino said.

"I'm getting interested. Do you remember what it said or not?"

"I wrote it down. It says 'Abbott and Fillmore. Domestic Investigations. Discreet. Confidential.' "

So Abbott was a divorce peeper. I hadn't remembered that about him. Paul had really picked the wrong guy, but he probably thought "domestic investigations" meant those conducted within the borders of the United States.

"Did you talk to Fillmore?" I asked.

"Yeah. He had a lot to say when I mentioned the hanging. Of course, he had to check me out first, but he told me plenty."

"For example."

"For example, he and another guy went to Picketville to scope things out. He doesn't think there was any suicide. He thinks somebody killed Abbott on purpose."

"Did he find out anything?"

"No. The sheriff basically ran him out of town before he could get started good. The sheriff told him not to nose around in things he didn't know anything about, and he told him that he'd let him know when the investigation was closed."

"And did he?"

"Not yet. Fillmore calls him every few days, though. The sheriff says he's still working on it."

That was news to me. Everyone had told me that the investigation by the sheriff's department had been concluded. Peavy was shining Fillmore on.

"Did Fillmore know what Abbott was working on?"

"Not really. Abbott wasn't exactly one of your reliable guys. He didn't file regular reports, and he didn't tell Fillmore who his client was in Picketville. Seems as if he and Fillmore weren't really partners. They just shared an office. I think if they'd been closer, Fillmore would still be in Picketville."

"Yeah," I said. "When someone kills your partner, you're supposed to do something about it."

"Huh?"

"Never mind."

"If you say so. Anyway, Fillmore said that he wasn't surprised Abbott got in trouble. He always operated right out in the open, with some stupid cover story about how he was working for the CIA or something."

Abbott didn't sound like a genius. Paul Lindeman should have called me. I couldn't have done any worse. But then if he'd called me, I might have been the one swinging from the bars in the Picketville jail.

"What about Gar Thornton?" I asked. "Did you get a line on him?"

"Not much of one. I still have a few contacts who help me out, though. They tell me he used to wrestle professionally under the name The Professor. He came in the ring dressed in an academic robe with a hood, like he had a Ph.D. from Harvard or somewhere. He wore one of those square hats with the tassel on it. He always carried a rolled-up diploma, too."

I tried to imagine Gar in academic regalia. I couldn't.

"I guess he lost a lot," I said.

"Yeah. But he was really a pretty good wrestler, and he got tired of being the loser all the time and got out of the game. He did promotions for athletic-related events for a while, like big card shows at the AstroHall and stuff like that, and then he just sort of dropped out of sight."

"He's good at that," I said. "He's just done it again. Is that it?"

"That's it. Any help?"

"I don't know yet," I told him.

There was something in what he said that was tickling at the back of my mind, but I couldn't bring it out to the front where I could get a look at it. Maybe later.

"Take care of my cat," I said.

"Don't worry about the cat. We're old buddies now. He doesn't even miss you."

He was probably right about that.

23

I'VE NEVER LIKED funerals. I suppose that some people do; I'm just not one of them.

I don't like the music, I don't like the flowers, I don't like the sad attempt to recall the happy moments of the dead person's life. I don't like the sermons, either. I don't like grief.

I don't like seeing the casket lowered into the ground, and I don't like watching the survivors tossing a handful of earth into the open hole.

Maybe I don't like all these things because they remind me of my own inevitable end. Anyway, for whatever reason, I was glad when the last words had been said and the cars began to leave the little oak-shaded cemetery near the funeral home where the visitation had been held.

It was a beautiful day. The rain had blown on down to the coast, leaving the sky a brilliantly washed blue, and the sun was pleasantly warm as it filtered through the oak leaves rustling above us. But the sweetness of the weather couldn't take away the chill of the burial.

After the minister had given his final words of comfort

to Anne and Red and had walked away, there was no one left at the grave except for the funeral director, who was standing at a discreet distance away, Anne, Red, me, and Lance.

The two men who were going to fill in the grave were sitting on the other side of the cemetery, waiting patiently in the shade of their backhoe.

Lance was standing next to Anne, too close to her, I thought. She was dry-eyed now, though she had wept openly during the service.

Red had wept, too, but he'd tried not to let anyone see him. He'd kept his head down and brushed at his eyes with the back of his hand.

Now he came over to me and said, "Smith, I want to get that bastard Gar. Him and Evans. They're the ones that put my boy in the ground."

"We don't know that, Red. I wish I could say we did."

He shook his head. "I thought you were different," he said. "I thought you weren't like Peavy and Denbow, but I guess you are. You're scared of Evans. You're afraid of what Gar might do to you."

I thought he was misjudging me, but to tell the truth, I wasn't exactly looking forward with eager anticipation to meeting Gar again. I looked over to where Anne and Lance were talking, their heads together.

"I'm sorry to be a disappointment to you," I told Red.

He shook his head. "Hell, I didn't mean all that. I know you're doin' the best you can. It's just that you're up against too much. You goin' back to Galveston now?"

"Not yet. But soon."

Maybe even sooner than I wanted to. Before the funeral service Lance had called me aside for a little talk.

"I think we can forget your job here, Tru," he said. "I'm pretty sure it was York who killed my bird. I'm going to pay you well for what you've done, but you can go on back to Galveston any time now."

"I think you're wrong," I said. "I don't think York killed Lindeman, and he didn't kill your bird, either."

"Do you have any proof of that?"

I didn't, of course. "It's just a feeling I have."

"Well, feelings don't count for much in a court of law, do they?"

"I guess not."

"I know not. I appreciate your help, but I think it's best that we forget the whole thing now."

And as far as Lance was concerned, that was that.

Not as far as I was concerned, however.

I spoke to Anne again, and left the cemetery. First I went by the Inn to change out of the cheap shirt and tie I'd bought for the funeral. Then I drove to the jail.

"YOU WANT TO talk to York?" Peavy said. "What makes you think I'll let you?"

"Because you like me?"

He almost smiled. "Not hardly."

"Because there's no real reason not to?"

He thought about it. "Oh, hell. Why not?"

HE EVEN LET us sit in the interrogation room, which I assumed was bugged. I imagined Peavy sitting in his office, leaning back in his chair and listening to every word York and I said.

If that was true, I didn't care. I wasn't going to say anything I didn't want Peavy to hear.

York didn't look good in the jailhouse jumpsuit. Orange wasn't his color. He also didn't look as if he'd slept much the previous night, and he probably hadn't eaten well, either.

"You've got to get me out of here, Smith," he said as soon as he sat down in the rickety wooden chair across the table from me. "I can't stand another day of this place."

I thought he could probably stand a lot more than he thought he could. He was about to find out, since there was no way I could get him out.

"What about a lawyer?" I asked. "The judge will set your bond today, and then maybe you can go home."

"I've got a good lawyer, but he says they're going to ask that no bond be set because this is a murder case. He says I might have to stay here for weeks—until the trial."

"You'll have to go before the grand jury first. They'll no-bill you unless the evidence against you is better than I think it is."

York stood up and walked nervously around the room. When he came back to the chair and sat down, he said, "It's better than you think it is. To tell the truth, it looks pretty bad."

I said that he was right, and that he shouldn't have knocked Denbow down and tried to get away.

"What would you have done?" he asked. "I knew I was innocent, and the last man they got into this stupid jail of theirs wound up hanging from the bars. I was afraid the same thing would happen to me."

I wasn't sure he'd actually been thinking that clearly. He was the kind of guy who liked to squeeze your hand when he shook it; maybe he thought he could actually overpower Denbow and get away with it.

"But that's not all," York said. "There's something else, something worse."

I was a little surprised at that. I said, "You want to tell me about it?"

He didn't, but he went ahead. I guess he didn't see any way out of it, not if he wanted my help.

"I had a crush on Anne," he said. "A foolish, adolescent crush, that's all it was. I can see that now."

"That's not evidence," I said.

"Oh, it's a lot worse than that. I kept a diary. They found it when they searched my house."

That could be pretty bad, all right, depending on what he'd written down.

"Lots of birders keep diaries," I said. "They write down all the birds they've seen. Or they have a checklist. They like to keep score."

"I had a checklist," York said, "just like everybody else. But the diary was different. I put my thoughts about Anne in there."

That was bad, all right.

"And I put my thoughts about Paul in there, too," he continued. "I said something about how nice it would be if Paul weren't around any longer."

That was even worse. York wasn't as smart as I'd thought, but then a man in love does stupid things sometimes. I'd been in love with Anne myself, once, and I thought I might be half in love with her still. So I couldn't really blame York for his stupidity.

"That doesn't sound good," I admitted, "but it's not proof of anything. Everyone's wished something like that at one time or another. If your lawyer's any good, the judge will set bond, and you'll be out of here before long. That's not what you have to worry about."

He didn't look relieved. "What do I have to worry about, then?"

"Are you guilty?"

"Of course not. This is the most ridiculous thing that I can imagine happening. First of all, I wasn't speeding when I was stopped."

"Are you sure?"

He sat back down and said, "Of course I am. I *never* speed. That's one of the things I pride myself on—obeying the traffic laws. I know how dangerous it is to drive too fast on some residential street, where a child can run out from between two parked cars when you least expect it."

"Then why did Denbow stop you?"

"You'll have to ask Deputy Denbow that question." His mouth twisted when he said "deputy." "But I think he stopped me because he knew that shotgun was in my backseat."

"That's another thing I wanted to know. How did that shotgun get there?"

"I don't have any idea. It's certainly not *my* shotgun. I hate guns. I would never allow one in my house, much less in my car."

He sounded as if he were telling the truth. I remembered the contempt in his voice when he asked me if I was a gun nut during our first conversation.

"So you think someone put the gun in your car?"

"It has to be that way. Someone's trying to blame me for the murder."

"They can't do it with the shotgun. That's another thing you don't have to worry about. They can't prove it was the one used in the murder. It may look suspicious, but that's all. Your lawyer will know all that."

For the first time, his eyes showed a glimmer of hope.

"Are you sure?" he asked.

"I'm sure. Ordinary rifles leave distinctive markings on bullets fired from them. Shotguns don't. You may have to spend another night in here, but that's the worst you can expect."

"Thank God." He looked thoughtful. "Does Anne know about this?"

I nodded.

"I was afraid of that. I was a fool to behave the way I did about her. But the truth is, she encouraged me."

To think I'd been feeling sorry for him. I wanted to lean across the table and hit him.

"Don't talk about Anne like that," I said.

He smiled a thin smile. "She gets to you, too, doesn't she?" I stood up. "I don't like you much, York. I'm beginning to hope you're guilty."

"Well, I'm not."

"Maybe not," I said, "but you're an asshole."

"And you're an uncouth ruffian."

He had me there, so I decided that it was time to leave. I walked to the door and knocked for the jailer. When he opened the door, I turned and said to York, "I may be an uncouth ruffian, but you're the one in jail for murder."

It was childish, I admit, but at least I got in the last word. Or if I didn't, I couldn't hear his answer. I slammed the door shut too hard.

Nobody ever said I was perfect.

IF PEAVY HAD been listening to my conversation with York, he didn't let on.

"York break down and confess?" he asked when I walked back into his office.

"No. He says it's all a frame. He says the shotgun was planted. He also says that he wasn't speeding when Denbow stopped him."

"Now why would he say a thing like that? It's his word against a law officer's, and you know who a judge and jury is going to believe."

"When I talked to you last night, you seemed pretty sure that you'd find something in York's house. What was it that gave you that idea?"

"I've got a sense for these things," Peavy said. "I've been a lawman for a long time."

If I hadn't known better, I might have thought there was an undertone of irony in his voice. But I knew better.

I also knew that I wasn't going to get anything else out of Peavy, but I gave it a try.

"What about Denbow? I'd like to talk to him about this."

Peavy's chair squeaked. It was a sound that for some reason was beginning to annoy me.

"You don't have any business here, Smith," Peavy said. "I've told you that before, and I don't want you messing around here anymore. You'd better just go on back where you came from. Either that, or you might get stopped for speeding."

That undertone of almost irony again.

"I'm just here visiting with Red Lindeman," I said. "That's all."

"It'd better be," Peavy said.

24

I DROVE OUT to Lance Garrison's ranch. Lance wasn't there, but Red was. That was fine with me. It was Red who I wanted to see.

He was sitting in a lawn chair in the shade of the pecan trees growing in front of the ranch house. The webbing on his lawn chair was in much better shape than the webbing on mine. He wasn't doing anything in particular, just looking out over the prairie grasses that were waving in the breeze. He didn't get up when I stopped the truck and got out, so I walked over to him. I didn't say anything. I just stood there beside him for a while, and we both stared into the distance.

After a minute or so had gone by, he said, "We never did get you a look at those prairie chickens you came out here to see, did we?"

"No, we never did get around to that. I don't guess it makes much difference now."

He reached down and got his crutches off the ground where they were lying.

"You oughta see 'em," he said as he got to his feet, balancing on the crutches. "That's what you came for, and it's a sight that not too many people can claim to have seen. Not these days, anyway. Come on."

He started toward my truck, and I followed.

"Wait a minute," Red said. "You might need some binoculars. I cleaned 'em up. They're on a little table just inside the front door."

I fetched the binoculars. When I got back to the truck, Red was already inside. He said, "Don't go the way we went the first time. The chickens won't be up around that marsh."

He pointed out a rutted road that led off through the tall grass, then disappeared. I headed the Chevy down it. We wound through the fields for what must have been a mile before he told me to stop the truck.

"Is this the spot?" I asked.

"Nope. We gotta walk from here. Truck'd just scare 'em if they're out there."

"How far?" I asked, thinking of the crutches even though he seemed to be able to maneuver very well on them.

"Depends." He opened the door and got out. "You comin' or not?"

"I'm coming."

I got out of the truck and walked around to where he was standing.

"The thing is," he said, "sometimes they're on the ground, and sometimes they're not. If they are, it's a sight to see, I'll tell you."

He started off awkwardly down the left-hand rut, and I walked on his right. It wasn't easy going for the crutches because the rut was narrow, but he didn't appear to be in any danger of falling.

"I read in a book once," he said, "that in the old days hunters used to come down here from central Texas and shoot prairie chickens for days at a time. They'd have 'em a contest, shoot from daylight till dark and pile up the dead birds for somebody to count. Most dead birds took the prize. Piles got as high as a tall man's waist. Sometimes, if it got to be too much trouble to bring in a whole bird, they'd just cut the heads off and bring in those instead. The whole prairie'd be covered with dead birds. They just left 'em there for the buzzards to eat. Now you can't hardly find a single chicken, even if you're lookin' for it."

I tried to picture a scene like the one he described, but I couldn't quite conjure it up. It wasn't that I was too sensitive for the idea of the slaughter; I just couldn't imagine the number of birds that must have been involved.

We walked on for another hundred yards and I said, "How hard would it be for someone to get on this land and locate the birds without being seen?"

"Pretty hard. Oh, somebody could get on the property easy enough. It's got a lot of miles of fence, and that's easy to cross. But findin' the birds is something else. You gotta know where to look."

"Martin York would have known, wouldn't he?"

"Yeah, old Martin was a good buddy of Lance's. Lance told me to take him out to see the birds, and I did it a couple of times. But I don't think he'd kill one."

I told him what I'd learned from York, about his feelings for Anne and his speculations about Paul.

Red shook his head stubbornly. "I still don't believe he'd kill a bird, much less Paul. He didn't have the gumption for something like that."

I thought about the way York had tried to crush my hand. I thought he had more gumption than Red was willing to give him credit for.

I had walked on for a few steps before I realized that Red wasn't beside me. I looked back, and he held up a hand.

"Listen," he said.

At first I didn't hear anything except the breeze rustling through the grasses, but then I heard something that sounded a little like someone saying "boo" over and over. I looked back at Red.

"That's them," he said. "Couple of 'em are boomin'. Let's be quiet now and we can get close enough to see 'em."

We walked along the ruts in silence for several yards. The road made a slight curve, and when we rounded it, I could see the birds about a hundred yards ahead of us.

There were two of them in a small clearing, both of them, I assumed, males. I brought up the binoculars that were hanging around my neck and focused in.

They were standing several yards apart, making their peculiar booming sound. Their orange neck sacs, bright in the sun, were blown up tight, like rubber balls. As I watched, they pattered their feet rapidly up and down, then charged one another, holding their tails and neck ruffs up while their wing tips nearly touched the ground. They ran together, then bounced back harmlessly and started the process all over again.

I watched for two or three minutes, after which one of the birds seemed to lose interest. He walked off into the grass, leaving the other alone. The remaining bird stayed where he was, having a wonderful time all by himself, flapping his wings, kicking dust, and chortling away.

"He can keep that up for as long as you want to watch him," Red said.

I lowered the binoculars. "Why would anybody want to kill one?"

"You got me there. Why would anybody want to kill a man?"

It's a pretty sad commentary on the state of my mind that I could think of more answers to his question than to my own.

"They're a pretty sight, though," Red said. "I'm glad you got to see 'em. You ready to go back to the house now?"

I looked down the road at the bird, who was still capering around, proclaiming that at least one spot of ground was indisputably his. I thought of hundreds of others like him, thousands, all booming and frisking on a perfect spring day. It was a sight I wasn't likely ever to see. Neither was anyone else for that matter.

I turned back to Red. "Let's go," I said.

AS WE DROVE toward the house, I told Red that Lance wanted me to go back to Galveston.

"I've got a mind to hire you, myself," Red said. "How much do you charge a day?"

"I don't think Sheriff Peavy would take it very well if I meddled in this," I said. "He hinted that I might find myself in the jail with York."

"You afraid of Peavy?"

"Not really. But he could make things tough if I tried to get around him."

"Guess he could, at that. But you know that Evans killed Paul. Him and that damn Gar. But Peavy won't touch either one of 'em. He didn't do anything to Evans about that airplane, and he's sure not gonna put a buddy in jail."

Red was probably right. I didn't see much that I could do about it, but I said, "I could stick around for a day or two, just to see how things go. I think Peavy will leave me alone as long as I stay out of his way."

"I'd appreciate it," Red said. "Anne would, too."

"I should go by and talk to Anne," I said. "There might be some things she could tell me that would help. Maybe Paul had some enemies that we don't even know about."

Red shook his head. "Nope. Ever'body liked Paul. Not an enemy in the world."

He'd had at least one, but there was no need to mention that.

"Besides," Red said, "Anne's not here. She told me that she was goin' out of town right after the funeral. She didn't want to stay in the house and be reminded of Paul all the time."

That sounded like a good idea. "Where did she go?"

"Galveston. She likes it down there on that island."

We were nearly to the house now. "Want to go on up to the marsh?" Red asked. "Might be a gator up there today. Lance says you like gators."

It was the mention of gators that jolted something loose in my head. It was almost like looking at one of those pictures that seem to be nothing more than a bunch of squiggles until you focus your eyes exactly right. When you do that, the picture suddenly resolves itself into what appears to be a three-dimensional image of a dinosaur or a flying saucer. You begin by looking at one thing, and suddenly you find yourself looking at something else entirely.

It had been that way with Fred Benton's murdered alligator. I'd gone into that case thinking that I was looking for whoever had killed a big, leathery reptile. But it hadn't been about the alligator at all, not when all was said and done.

I'd sensed almost from the beginning that this case hadn't been about a dead bird, either, but I hadn't been able to figure out anything else that it could have involved. It was different now, and I found myself remembering earlier sounds and earlier conversations in which things were said that at the time I hadn't paid enough attention to. Now things that had gone right past me took on a dark significance.

I was still vague on a lot of the details, but if I could get the right people to talk to me, a few phone calls and a little conversation might clear most things up.

I didn't like what I was thinking. I even hoped I was wrong. But I doubted that I was.

I parked the truck in front of the house and told Red that I needed to make a few calls. A couple of them would be long-distance.

"Be my guest," he said. "I don't pay the bills."

I'd already thought of that. I told him that it wouldn't take me long and that I'd appreciate it if he stayed out in the yard while I talked.

"You don't have to worry about that. I won't be buttin' into your business. I'll be happy right over there in that chair."

He crutched over to the lawn chair, and I went inside to make my calls.

An hour later, I was on my way back to Galveston.

25

WHEN I GOT back to the Island, I fed Nameless and called Lance. Then I called Dino.

"What now?" he asked. "You want some more information, or are you just homesick?"

"I'm not homesick," I said. "I'm home."

I was sitting in my broken recliner, listening to the Shirelles on CD. They were singing about a boy they'd met on Sunday and missed on Monday.

"You wrapped that up pretty quick," he said.

"It's not wrapped up yet," I said. "I have to talk to Lance first. There are a couple of more things I have to find out before I can say it's finished."

"Lance is back here on the Island?"

"Yeah. I just called him."

"You called him first?"

"Jealousy is such an ugly emotion," I said.

"It sure is. How's my cat?"

"You can't get to me that way. Nameless was overjoyed to see me."

"I bet he was."

"Wagged his tail like a dog. Wiggled all over."

"You got a Polaroid of that? I'd like to see it."

"Maybe I exaggerated. I get a little giddy when I figure something out. You want to ride out to Lance's with me?"

He didn't hesitate. "Nope."

"Well, come anyway. You're the one who got me into all this."

"There's this great infomercial on right now. It's the best one they have, the one about Touchless car wax. I love that little English guy who wears the bow tie."

"Bow ties turn you on?"

"You know what I mean."

"I guess I do," I said. "I guess if some little Englishman in a bow tie means more to you than our lifelong friendship, you really should stay there and watch your show. Besides, if you watch it, you won't have to leave the house."

"You really are a wiseass, you know that?"

"You might be surprised at how often I've heard that lately."

"Not likely. But what the hell. I'll be there in half an hour."

"I'll be waiting," I said.

IT WAS, IN the words of one of my favorite philosophers, déjà vu all over again. I was sitting in the same lawn chair, reading the same book, when Dino drove up in his '81 Pontiac. The only difference was that the Pontiac was much cleaner.

"You waxed the car," I said when Dino got out.

"Yeah. I bought some stuff I saw on TV. Not Touchless, though. Looks good, right?"

"Like new."

He glanced at *Tobacco Road*. "That's a pretty short book. I thought you'd be finished by now."

"I've been busy."

While we were talking, Nameless came out of the oleanders. He saw Dino and walked over, arching his back and rubbing against Dino's leg.

"See what I mean?" Dino said.

"He thinks you're here to feed him," I said. "He just ate, though."

"I guess I won't feed him then."

Nameless said "Mowrr" and walked over to me. He rubbed against my leg and looked up at me.

"Fickle," Dino said. "That's what he is. He likes that cat food better than he likes anybody."

I marked my place in the book and stood up. "Are you ready to go see Lance?"

Dino nodded. He was still looking at Nameless, who was wandering back into the oleanders.

"Why don't we go in your car?" I said. "That's what we did last time."

Dino shrugged. "Sure. This gonna take long?"

"I don't think so."

"Good. They're gonna show that Touchless thing again in a couple of hours. I'd like to see it."

"No promises," I said.

"Yeah," he said. "That's what I thought."

IT WAS NEARLY sunset when we got to Lance's house, the low light silvering the water in the bay and reddening the sky, low in the west. Most of the palm trees were in shadow. Lance's Acura was parked under the overhang. The MR-3 was there, too.

"You sure you want to do this?" Dino asked before we started up the stairs.

I'd told him most of the story on the way. "Hey, it's the

job. He said he wanted to know who killed his prairie chicken, and I'm going to tell him."

"He's not going to like it."

"I know that. But I've got you to back me up."

"Right."

I rang the doorbell, and in a few seconds Lance opened the door.

"Good to see you again, Tru," he said. "You, too, Dino. Come on in."

He had on his Birkenstocks again, and the cotton slacks and sports shirt. Not the same slacks and shirt he'd been wearing on my earlier visit, but the same brand, right down to the polo player on the shirt. He smiled as he led us into the room with the hardwood floors and all the glass.

"Everybody have a seat," he said.

Dino sat on the couch, and Lance sat beside him. I took the wooden rocker.

When we were more or less comfortable, Lance said, "You were in a pretty big hurry to see me, Tru. I guess you've come for your check. I've already got it made out."

He reached into his shirt pocket and brought out a light green check folded in half. He handed it to me, and I stuck it in the pocket of my jeans without looking at it.

"Too bad about Martin York," Lance said. "I would never have thought he'd kill a sparrow, much less a prairie chicken. Not to mention a human being."

"He didn't kill anybody," I said.

Lance sat up straight on the couch. "What? Has he been released from jail?"

"Not yet, but it's just a matter of time. He didn't have anything to do with killing anyone."

Lance looked as if he didn't believe me. "You're sure about that?"

"Pretty sure. You want to hear about it?"

"That's what I paid you for. I gave you the check. You give me a report."

"That sounds fair," I said.

I looked out through the windows at the sunset. It was going to be spectacular.

"I'm going to have to go at the story in a roundabout way," I said.

Lance didn't look pleased about that. "Why?"

"Because that's the way it plays out. I went to Picketville to find out who killed your bird, but I finally figured out that the bird was just a part of something else, something that started a few weeks before."

"And what was that?" Lance asked.

"The murder of a man named Lloyd Abbott."

"Am I supposed to know about him?"

"He's the man who supposedly hanged himself in his jail cell in Picketville."

"Oh. I think I heard something about that." Lance leaned back on the cushions of the couch. "It was a suicide, though, not murder."

"That's what the sheriff told everyone, but it was murder. And the sheriff knew it all along."

"You mean that he covered it up? Was he involved?"

"No," I said. "I thought he was for a while, but he wasn't." I paused. "It was Gar Thornton who killed Abbott."

"Gar? That big guy who's Ralph's bodyguard?"

"That's the one."

Lance looked thoughtful. "You know, I thought all along it was probably Evans. He never did like the idea that I was getting government money to support that prairie chicken project."

"Evans didn't kill the bird," I said. "And he didn't tell Gar to kill Abbott. I think the murder was just an accident. Gar might have meant to scare Abbott, but he didn't mean to kill him."

"There was something about a fight in a bar," Lance said. "I remember now. Gar might have gone to the jail to finish the job."

"It wasn't that, either."

"What was it, then?"

"I'll tell you," I said. "I should have figured it out when I remembered that Abbott did divorces. I found out that Paul Lindeman had hired him, but I thought he'd hired him to investigate some kind of irregularities in the sheriff's office. That's what I was led to believe, anyway. But Paul wasn't stupid. He hired Abbott to do exactly what he advertised that he was good at—divorce work."

"What does that have to do with me?" Lance asked.

"You were having an affair with Paul's wife. With Anne," I said. My throat was tight. I didn't want to say her name, and I had to force the words out.

Lance smiled, but his smile was as forced as my words had been. "You're kidding."

"No," I said. "All the signs were there. Her visits to Galveston, the way you hovered around her at her house and at the funeral. Anybody a little less stupid than me would have caught on a lot faster. Besides, I talked to Abbott's partner. He told me all about it."

That was a lie, but Lance wouldn't know it. Fillmore hadn't told me the name of Abbott's client because he didn't have any idea who it was. Abbott was secretive about such things. There was probably a record on Abbott's computer, but Fillmore didn't know the password. I'd called Johnny and arranged a visit to see if we could crack the code.

I'd talked to Peavy, too, telling him some of what I knew or had guessed. Peavy admitted that he knew Abbott's death wasn't an accident and that he was sure Gar was responsible. He wasn't covering it up, however; he was still trying to prove it. That's why he wanted me out of the way, and it was for the same reason he'd wanted Fillmore out of the way earlier.

"Abbott was a hotdog," I said. "He liked to use covers that called attention to him. The CIA was one of his favorites. The IRS was another. My guess is that when he came to town posing as someone from Internal Revenue, you got pretty scared. You have a shaky investment or two, so you wanted Gar to find out more about him. He did, but in the process, he killed him."

"Hold on," Lance said. "Gar doesn't work for me. He works for Ralph Evans, remember?"

"That might be what Evans thinks. I don't."

"That's the silliest thing I ever heard," Lance said.

"Then maybe you don't want to hear the rest."

"Oh, hell. Why not? Go ahead."

"All right. You were worried about the real IRS because of Evans. When Abbott showed up, you thought maybe the government objected to Evans's program, and you were the target. Disgrace you, and Evans would be discredited, too. So you wanted to get rid of him. But you didn't. His revenues were falling and the advertisers were dropping away, but he stayed on the air, and he told me he didn't have a thing to worry about. Why? Because he knew about the affair."

"You're an idiot."

"No. I asked Evans about it this afternoon. He as much as admitted it. So you wanted to get rid of him even more. How? Blame him for killing the prairie chicken, and then claim that anything he said was sour grapes from a man who'd killed an endangered bird. You'd heard about me and the alligator. You figured you could hire me, throw a few hundred clues in my lap, and I'd frame Evans for you."

"But you didn't."

"No. The clues weren't evidence. You tried to solidify the frame by having Gar run York's birding friends, the Greers, off the road. They blamed that on Evans, naturally. You even had Gar fly the plane while you strafed me and Red."

Lance stood up. "Wait a minute. You know better than that. I was in Houston when that happened."

I rocked back and forth slowly in the wooden chair. The sun was lowering itself behind a cloud bank and the shadows were gathering over the bay.

"No, you weren't," I said. "I talked to your secretary this afternoon. I have to admit that I used Peavy's name instead of my own. She admitted that you weren't in a meeting when I called about the plane. She'd just been told to say that."

"But I called you. You remember that."

"You called, all right. On a cellular phone. You called her first, then me. It took me a while to figure out that the squealing I heard wasn't your desk chair. It was the hangar door at Evans's place."

"Nobody will ever believe any of this."

"Peavy will. He was going slow on Gar because he thought Gar worked for Evans, and Evans and Peavy are pals. But Peavy had found out that Gar worked for you. From Paul. So Peavy's pretty sure you killed Paul, or had Gar do it. I vote for Gar. You wouldn't have the nerve to do it yourself."

"But they found the shotgun in York's car!"

"Where you put it. You were parked beside him at Anne's house, and no one in Picketville locks a car. It would have been easy to stick the shotgun in the backseat. Then you called Denbow and mentioned the gun. He stopped York for speeding to have an excuse to look in the car. You even knew about York's diary, because he'd mentioned it to Anne. Another anonymous call took care of that part of things."

"But why would I try to frame York? I thought you said I was trying to frame Evans."

"The Evans frame didn't work, or it didn't work fast enough. I was stupid, but I wasn't that stupid. So you decided to try something else. Any old frame would do, if you could make it fit."

Lance took a few steps toward my chair. "Red's the one who asked for you. It wasn't my idea."

"That's another lie. When we were on our way to Evans's land, Red said that he hadn't seen Fred Benton in years. They'd never discussed me and the alligator. And Red also told me that you were the one who suggested where we should look for the crop duster. If I'd been thinking straight, I'd have figured things out then. You wanted me because you figured I was still the stupid guy who broke your nose when we were in high school."

"If any of this is true—any of it—why didn't Paul tell you?"

"Because he knew I was working for you."

"Fine. So if he kept his mouth shut, why did I have him killed?"

"I think it was because he'd found out the truth about Gar's work for you. He knew that Gar had killed Abbott, and he knew that the IRS agent pose had you worried. He must have known that Gar used to work shows at the AstroHall, and you once had a piece of the Astros. You could easily have met Gar, and it wouldn't have been hard for Paul to make the connection. He was looking into it, and he was letting Tony Lopez help out. Lopez was lucky. He wasn't getting anywhere."

Lance stopped a few feet from me. "It's not true. None of it's true. There's no proof of any of it."

"Not unless you count the proof of your affair with Anne. I can talk to your neighbors about that. I imagine it won't be hard to prove that she stayed here rather than at a motel when she visited Galveston. And then there's Gar. He's even more stupid than I was. He's the one who's going to take the fall for you."

"No, he's not," Gar said, stepping into the room from the hallway.

26

GAR LOOKED PRETTY much the same as ever, except that he wasn't wearing his cap. His hair was slicked back, and he had a rubber band around his stubby ponytail.

His voice was the surprise. It was a sweet tenor that would have sounded great singing lead in a doo-wop group on a street corner in Brooklyn somewhere around 1957.

"I didn't see your truck outside," I said.

"I don't park here," Gar said.

"Did you hear everything he said?" Lance asked.

"Sure. What do you want me to do about it?"

"That's a problem," Lance said. "If you'd stayed in the other room, it might not have been."

"He knows too much. He can cause us a lot of trouble. We have to take care of him."

Dino, who had been listening silently to all of this, stood up and said, "Well, I sure as hell don't know anything. If nobody minds, I'll just get out of here and head for home. There's a TV show I want to watch."

"I don't think so," Lance said.

"You might as well let him go," I said. "And me, for that matter. I told Peavy everything. He'll take care of Gar soon enough, and he'll be able to bring you into it by then, too, even if Gar's a stand-up guy."

Lance didn't seem worried. "Maybe you told Peavy, maybe not. Whatever happens, you won't be around to see it." He nodded in my direction. "Get rid of them, Gar. I don't care how you do it. Feed them to the crabs if you want to."

"That's not very hospitable," I said as Gar smiled and started toward me. "And I don't think Gar can handle both me and Dino."

Lance smiled, too, and said, "We'll see, won't we?"

I stood up, reached under my sweatshirt, and pulled out my little Mauser.

"I thought Gar might be here," I said. "So I came prepared."

"Guns don't scare Gar," Lance said.

My turn to smile. "I wasn't planning to shoot Gar. But if he comes any closer, I'm going to shoot you."

A voice from the hallway said, "You're not going to shoot anyone, Tru."

Anne walked into the room. She looked as beautiful as ever except for the fact that she was holding a twelve-gauge automatic shotgun, and she looked as if she knew how to use it. I wondered if it was the gun that had killed Paul or a different one, not that it mattered.

Seeing her there depressed me as much as anything else that had happened in the last few days. There was no little man inside my chest slugging my heart with a sledgehammer this time, just a feeling like the kind you get when a close friend dies.

She'd as much as told me that there was nothing left between her and Paul, even while she was telling me that she still loved him, and of course I'd believed what I wanted to believe. That was what hurt.

That, and the fact that she'd run to Lance again. She always seemed to wind up with Lance.

I should have seen through her from the first, of course, but my old feelings for her got in the way. There's nothing quite as debilitating as the ghost of a memory, especially the memory of adolescent love.

"Why don't you put down the pistol, Tru?" Lance said. "You could shoot me, I suppose, but what good would it do?"

He had a point. I laid the pistol on the floor, and Anne walked over to stand beside him. He took the shotgun from her and said, "I'm sorry things ended up like this, Tru."

"I'll bet." He didn't sound sorry to me.

"I'm not making a joke," he said. "I really am sorry. Anne told me that I shouldn't try to do things the hard way. But I had a dead man to explain away. I knew Peavy wasn't satisfied with things, and I knew Paul was meddling. If you'd just given Evans to them, things would have been fine."

"Sure. Peachy. I'd like to know two more things, by the way."

"What's that?"

"Did you really call Paul the night he died, or did Anne just say there'd been a call?"

"What difference does that make?"

"None, I guess."

Except to me. I wondered if she'd coldly sent him to his death or whether she'd just let Lance or Gar summon him there.

"Fine. What's the second thing?"

"Are you still pissed off because I broke your nose?"

Dino grinned at that, but Lance didn't. He said, "Gar, I think you'd better take them downstairs and put them in the car. You can dispose of them elsewhere. I don't want to mess up the decor in here. They should have some sort of tragic accident that won't reflect on me. A car wreck would be nice."

Everyone had been watching me closely because I was the one nearest the pistol. Dino had managed to slide a step toward Lance, which put him close enough to make a jump for the shotgun. As soon as Gar started toward me, Dino made his move.

He lunged at the shotgun and got both hands around the barrel, twisting it upward just as the gun exploded, sending a tight pattern of shot into the ceiling, which erupted into a Sheetrock shower.

I dived for the Mauser and got my fingers on it, but Gar was even quicker than I'd remembered. He landed on me like a hummer with a load of bricks. I collapsed beneath him like a paper bag, and the pistol skittered under the couch.

I couldn't get my breath with Gar on top of me, and I'm sure he knew it. To make things worse, he got an arm around my throat and began to choke me.

I felt my head swelling up like a prairie chicken's neck sac. It was probably about the same color, too. I was glad I couldn't see it.

I figured I had about ten seconds left to live, maybe less. There was nothing at all I could do to save myself.

I tried to think some profound thought to go out on, but it was no use. All I could think of was that Evelyn would probably take care of Nameless if Dino was killed, too.

I was seeing bright yellow lights behind my eyelids and things were just about to go completely black when I heard something that sounded like a wooden bat connecting for a solid base hit.

The pressure around my neck was gone, and I sucked in huge gasps of air.

The shotgun went off again, and I heard glass breaking. Then I heard Dino yell.

I opened my eyes. Everything was blurry, but I could see that Gar had knocked Dino down and was kneeling on his chest. While I watched, he hit him twice, his fist moving so rapidly that I could hardly follow it.

I didn't know where the shotgun was, or Lance, or Anne, but I knew I had to try to help Dino. I got up and tried to suck in some air. I got a little, but I got a lot of Sheetrock dust, too. Coughing and sneezing, I made a drunken leap at Gar, who was so surprised to see me coming that he almost didn't have time to react.

"Almost" is the key word. He got up a hand and batted me to one side, but I somehow managed to stick a finger in his eye. I gave a hard twist and tried to pop his eyeball out, but I didn't succeed. He yelled, though, and I knew that I'd hurt him.

He leaned back, shouting something I couldn't quite understand, then rolled to his feet and aimed a kick at my head.

I scrambled out of the way, and Dino got up. He put his head down and ran straight at Gar, who had his hands over his eye.

Blood was running down his cheek. I thought at first it was coming from his eye, but then I noticed a gash on his forehead. Dino must have hit him with the shotgun, but it hadn't slowed him down much.

While Gar pawed at his eye, Dino shoved him backward a few feet, and I got up to do what I could to help, which wasn't going to be much. I was still having trouble just trying to breathe.

Gar swung at Dino with one hand, but Dino dodged. The eye had slowed Gar down a bit. Or maybe the blow from the shotgun was finally bothering him.

Dino charged again, and this time I was right beside him.

"Shove the son of a bitch through the window," Dino said.

Gar was pounding at us with one oak-hard fist, but we

forced him slowly back, his shoes squeaking on the hardwood floor.

"Now!" Dino said. "Shove him!"

I shoved, and so did Dino. Gar stumbled backward a half step, tried to stop, couldn't, and crashed into the thick plate glass. In its original state it might have been strong enough to stop even Gar, but the noise I had heard a few seconds before was the sound of a shotgun blast striking the glass, which was now considerably weakened.

Gar went right on through, with a silvery, splintering crash. He was followed out into the late afternoon light by hundreds of slivers of glass that glittered like red-and-gold rain in the sunset light.

There was a loud thud when Gar hit the ground, but he didn't cry out. Glass jangled after him.

I stood for a second with my hands on my knees, and soon I could breathe a bit more easily. Then I turned to see what else had happened.

The shotgun was lying near an end table, where it had fallen after knocking off a lamp.

Lance was lying on the floor with Anne kneeling beside him.

"What happened to him?" I asked Dino.

Dino grinned. "I think I broke his nose," he said.

27

"W H AT I WA N T to know," Dino said the next day, "is
who killed the damn prairie chicken."

We were sitting in his living room watching TV. Or Dino
was watching. Even while we talked, he didn't take his eyes
off it. I was drinking a Big Red and trying to ignore the
infomercial about some kind of little bullet-shaped instru-
ment called "the Stimulator" that was supposed to relieve any
kind of pain you might have by administering a small electric
shock to whatever part of your body it was applied to.

I sort of wished I had one, actually. I had quite a few
places that I could try it out on.

"I don't know who killed the prairie chicken," I said. "But
it had to be either Lance or Anne. I don't know why I didn't
figure that out right from the beginning, and maybe I would
have if Red had told me how hard it was to catch a sight of
them. Whoever killed that bird had to know his way around
the ranch. Or *her* way around. Whoever it was had to be able
to find the birds and get close enough for a shot. Red could
have done it, but of course he didn't."

"What about that York guy?"

"He might have been able to do it, but he didn't have access to the ranch like Anne and Lance did. It had to be one of them. They did it to get me there, that's all."

"Too bad you didn't turn out to be quite as dumb as they thought."

"Ignorance is bliss," I said.

"I heard about that," Dino said. "I never really believed it, though."

I'd never really believed it, either, but I think my life would have been quite a bit more blissful if I'd never gone to Picketville, never seen Anne or Lance again.

"What do you think'll happen to them?" Dino asked.

"Depends on what Gar has to say when he gets out of traction."

"Could have been us in traction," Dino said. "Or in the morgue. You told me not to worry, that you had a pistol. Everything would be fine, you said."

"I was wrong."

"You can say that again."

"I was—"

"Hey, don't say it again. I was only kidding."

I shut my mouth, and Dino turned back to the TV set. After watching testimonials for a minute or so he said, "You think that thing really works?"

"I don't know. Right now I'd like to give it a try."

"Takes four to six weeks for shipping," Dino said. "Otherwise I'd call that 800 number right now."

"You know what?" I said.

"What?"

"You and Evelyn and Cathy and I ought to drive up and see Red one day soon, let him take us on a tour of the ranch. Those prairie chickens are really something to see. And it may be your last chance."

Dino didn't look at me. "It's a long way up there," he said.

"It's not so far. You wouldn't even have to get out of the car if you didn't want to."

"Too much wide-open space for me. You can probably see for miles."

"That's true," I said. "But these birds might not be around much longer. They might all disappear during our lifetime. You should have a look at them."

"I'll think about it," he said.

I let him think about it while I remembered the booming sound and the way the male bird's feet had pattered the ground, so fast that even through the binoculars they were nothing more than a blur.

Then I thought about Anne and Lance. I decided that I was right about one thing: People never change. Lance was a lot richer, but somewhere inside he was still a sneak who didn't want to get hurt and who sent someone like Gar to do his dirty work. Anne was still the girl who'd wanted more from life than someone like me or Paul Lindeman could give her.

And, of course, I was still their stooge.

The infomercial ended, and Dino used his complicated remote to turn off the TV set.

"How long would it take us to get there?" he asked.

"An hour and a half. About."

"And I wouldn't have to get out of the car?"

"Not if you didn't want to."

"Cathy might not want to have anything to do with you, the way you went chasing off after Anne."

"I've talked to Cathy. She'd love to go."

"Well," Dino said.

He turned the TV set back on. Dick Clark was hawking a set of CDs.

"You got those?" Dino asked.

"No. But it's a great set."

He put the remote on his coffee table and we watched a very short clip of Jerry Lee Lewis.

"I'll go," Dino said. "If Evelyn wants to."

"I've talked to her, too. She's ready anytime you are."

"Not today," he said.

"OK. Saturday?"

"Yeah. I guess. Tell me about those birds again."

He turned off the TV set, and I told him.